THE MAN
WITHOUT
QUALITIES

Also by Morris Berman

Social Change and Scientific Organization

Trilogy on human consciousness:
    The Reenchantment of the World
    Coming to Our Senses
    Wandering God: A Study in Nomadic Spirituality

Trilogy on the American empire:
    The Twilight of American Culture
    Dark Ages America: The Final Phase of Empire
    Why America Failed: The Roots of Imperial Decline

A Question of Values (essays)
Destiny (fiction)
Counting Blessings (poetry)
Spinning Straw Into Gold (memoir)

Praise for *The Man Without Qualities*

As much a work of philosophy as a novel, Morris Berman's *The Man Without Qualities* offers a new political orientation—None of the Above. In the aftermath of politics as usual, partisans of Berman's Dullness Institute can at last give a hearty Nietzschean laugh and say, "Workers of the World!... Relax!"

—Curtis White, author of *We, Robots*, *The Science Delusion*, *The Middlemind*, and *Memories of My Father Watching Television*

In *The Man Without Qualities*, renowned historian and cultural critic Morris Berman delves into the complex topic of authenticity with humor, warmth, and crisp prose. His protagonist, George Haskel, is a German lit professor who is bored with his life and especially with his unengaged students. Leaving academia behind, George embarks on a singular mission, to launch the Dullness Institute, in defiance of all that is endlessly competitive, needlessly greed-driven, and generally fake in the United States. To be dull, for George, is to shun the need to "project" and rather, to just "be." In doing so, the impact of George's vision and that of his colorful collective of like-minded friends and eventually millions of people, bid fair to alter the course of humanity. Berman's novel shines a skeptical light on how we are evolving and shows us a better, more authentic path.

—Nomi Prins, author of *It Takes a Pillage*, *All the Presidents' Bankers*, and other works

ISBN: 978-0-9883343-5-9
Library of Congress Control Number: 2016900210

The Oliver Arts & Open Press, LLC
2578 Broadway, Suite #102
New York, NY 10025
www.oliveropenpress.com

THE MAN
WITHOUT
QUALITIES

Morris Berman

THE OLIVER ARTS & OPEN PRESS

1.

It was when I hit seventy years of age that I decided to retire; that I had had enough. I had spent more than forty years as a professor of German literature, and truth be told, the classroom experience had long ceased to provide me with any thrills. My students were typically dull, and in any case sat in class staring into their laptops updating their Facebook profiles, or else texting on their smart phones. If I asked them what Rilke meant when he wrote, "You must change your life," they had no idea. Nothing much moved them, and by the time I reached seventy, nothing much moved me as well.

I didn't know how much longer I had to live; perhaps a few years at most. The members of my immediate family had all died in their seventies from heart-related disease, and as I was a bit overweight and had high cholesterol, I figured I would just follow the familial pattern. I was a bachelor, had no dependents, and had retired with enough to live on comfortably, so figured I would just spend the next few years traveling. It was something I always enjoyed.

Now I have to tell you that having been born in Europe (my parents immigrated to the United States when I was five), I could never quite adapt to the American way of life, and as

I grew older, I felt like I was an anthropologist observing a strange tribe. Americans, I quickly learned, were very interested in money; I wasn't. They were always striving for something; beyond getting tenure, which I obtained in my midthirties, I had no ambition at all. They worshipped celebrity, being famous, whereas I was content to be anonymous. The upper-middle classes were keen on self-improvement, on taking classes in sketching or Indian cooking, so as to make themselves "interesting"; this didn't attract me in the least. My favorite novel was the one by Robert Musil, *The Man Without Qualities,* and I liked the idea of moving through society without having any distinguishing characteristics. So when I retired, it struck me that it might be fun, in a kind of screwy way, to construct a story about myself as an infinitely dull person, and see what would happen if I were to interact with other people on that basis. My guess was that nothing would happen, but the idea still intrigued me. Had anyone undertaken such a peculiar project, and then written it up? I figured it was worth a shot.

Two months later I found myself in the old colonial town of Morelia, in Mexico, where I had rented a room. Every day, I would sit in the town square, drink coffee, and read an English or German novel from a small collection of books I had brought with me. On my fifth day there, I was approached by an American woman in her late forties, who wanted to sit at my table.

"Do you mind?" she asked, speaking to me in English. "All the other tables seem to be taken."

"No, not at all," I said, gesturing for her to sit down. This seemed like a good opportunity to practice dullness. I kept reading, while she ordered coffee and *pan dulce.*

"Are you a tourist?" she finally asked me.

"Yes, that's right," I told her; "I'm just traveling around Mexico to see what it's like."

"It's pretty good," she said; "I've been living here for five years." There was kind of a pause. "Do you live in the US?"

"Yes, just outside of Washington, DC." More pause.

"What do you do there, if I may ask?"

I put down my book. Clearly, I had hooked a fish. "I'm retired, actually, but I used to be a car salesman."

"And so now you decided to travel?" she wanted to know.

"Well, it's the only thing I've ever done that's been interesting. My basic interest in life has been money, and I got very good at making it. I mean, money by itself is not very interesting, I suppose; although it was to me. Along with alcohol, I have to admit; which is also not very interesting."

She laughed. "So you regard yourself as dull?"

I pretended to frown. "Well, I guess that to be an interesting person, you have to be interested in things that are interesting—you know, like art or literature or whatever. But I never was. My whole life has been devoted to money, alcohol, women, and travel. The travel part is interesting, I guess. But I'm the kind of person who rarely gets invited to dinner parties, because I don't say very much; and that's because I don't have very much to say." I shrugged. "I'm just being honest. I mean, I can tell you about my trip to Paris twenty years ago, but beyond stuff like that—well, I just draw a blank. In fact, my coworkers at the car dealership used to call me 'Mr. Blank.' I didn't mind; they were just telling it like it is. What do *you* do, by the way?"

"Oh, I'm retired as well," she said, "but I used to be an attorney. I worked in Los Angeles, in the area of intellectual property rights."

"Well, there you have it: I don't even know what intellectual property rights are."

"Oh, one band sues another band for stealing the melody line of one of their songs, and hires me to defend them. That kind of thing. I eventually got tired of it, moved down here. But tell me more about your own life. You say it was dull, but I don't find it all that boring, somehow." She flashed me a smile.

"Hmm," I said, pretending to reflect on my wasted years. "Well, when you are interested in money, work fourteen hours a day year in and year out, and have just a bit of luck, you can become very rich; which I did. So I own a large house in the Maryland suburbs, have two Mercedes, servants who take care of the property, that sort of thing. The alcohol part: you know, there are all these wine clubs and single-malt Scotch clubs in Washington, but I never bothered with that. I figured if I paid two grand for a bottle of wine, I would probably enjoy it, and I always did. And then the women: you'd think they wouldn't be interested in a dull dog like myself, but in my experience they are very interested in dull dogs with money, so that part of my life came pretty easy."

"So you were never in love, or were married, or had kids?" she asked.

"Never had any attraction for me, and frankly, I doubt that any of my girlfriends were in love with me either. Eventually, they all moved on, and I was OK with that."

"So who will inherit your vast wealth?" she smiled.

I faked a laugh. "I'm setting up a foundation dedicated to dullness. It will be called the Dullness Institute, and its job will be to teach people how to become boring. How to stop reading, give up their hobbies, end their relationships, and so on."

"Oh go on!" she said. "You know, I almost believed you."

"Here's the literature," I said, handing her a brochure. "It's still in the planning stage, of course, but this is the basic idea." This was a pamphlet I had printed up in the US before I left, outlining the basic goals and principles of a purported Dullness Institute. "We even have a web site," I boasted.

She read through the pamphlet with interest; I ordered another cappuccino, and lit a small cigar.

"You're quite mad, you know," she finally said, when she finished reading the literature. "Is that why I find you fascinating?"

I staged another laugh. "Well, you'd be the first. Usually it's because I'm filthy rich. Women can smell it, you know; it's a sixth sense with them."

"And a cynic to boot."

"Just speaking from experience," I shot back. "I mean, they aren't going to be attracted to me based on looks or personality; let's face it. Why don't we have dinner tonight?"

"So you can bore my pants off?" She winked.

"Well, *you* sure ain't dull," I told her.

Later, I reviewed the conversation in my mind. Had I succeeded or failed? But then, what, exactly, was my goal? To be dull? To be interesting? To be interesting by being dull? I seemed a bit confused about it all. But one thing I *was* sure of: I was enjoying being dull. I didn't particularly want to sleep with her (I didn't even know her name; we just agreed to meet at 8 P.M. at the same café). She was rather attractive, but I had had enough sex in my life. The "experiment" I was conducting, whatever it was, was much more exciting.

Her name was Alice, as it turned out. She was forty-eight years old. She had dark, shoulder-length hair, and rather round eyes, which were brown. She had done well in the intellectual property rights business in LA; a major lawsuit involving some hip-hop group had netted her a cool 2 million, after which she closed her office and moved down south. Why she was spending time with me was beyond my comprehension.

We met at the same café, and then wandered over to her favorite Mexican restaurant. I reflected that it was good that I wasn't angling to sleep with her, because it meant I could "blow it"—be as dull as I could manage, and just see what would happen. I began to think she must be right: I was mad as a hatter.

We ordered margaritas, and leaned back in our chairs. "So tell me about all these gold-diggers you slept with," she asked me conspiratorially.

"Oh," I said, "you don't really wanna know. Like me, most of them were dull, and to be honest, not especially attractive. In most cases it was just a business deal: I would spend money on them, and they would sleep with me in return. Nobody said it, but it was basically prostitution."

"And you never felt anything for any of them? Really?"

"Not that I remember," I replied. "You see, I'm fundamentally a practical guy. On the rare occasion that I go to a movie, and there's some romantic plot involved, I keep wondering what all the fuss is about. Are we really all so different? I don't think so. I think we're mostly interchangeable. One woman—or man, for that matter—is as good as another, in my opinion. I mean, does it really matter who is president? It's actually money that's running the show, no?"

She finished her margarita and I signaled the waiter for another round. "You've certainly got a point there," she said. "But seriously, haven't you ever been moved by something? A sunset, a poem, a home run at a baseball game?"

"I was forced to read poetry in high school; I haven't read a line of it since. And I hate baseball."

"OK, then; how about drugs?"

"Never touch the stuff. I'll tell you the one great rush I had in my life, though. It was about twelve years ago; some sheik from the Middle East bought no less than forty custom-built limousines. My commission came to 8 million dollars. Now that moved me, sister."

Alice sighed. The waiter came over; we ordered *pozole*, and chicken enchiladas. "Are you sure you're not really a nuclear physicist?" she asked me.

This time I laughed, for real. "I don't think I even know what an atom is," I told her.

"But you do have a passion for dullness, right? Where did *that* come from?"

"I'm not sure," I said, "but probably from watching Americans, from an early age. Everything is about shining, about standing out; wouldn't you agree? I remember all the kids in my high school trying to be better, trying to be special, trying to impress. It seemed exhausting; I didn't know how they could stand it. And then I went to college, and discovered it was worse. It was all about being cool. I dropped out after one semester. I had no interest in being cool. I just wanted to make money, which is what I proceeded to do. Being dull, not being cool, lifted a great burden off me. Really, dullness is where it's at, and that's what I want to promote with my Institute. Look," I continued, warming to the subject, "tell me what you do down here; what's your typical day like?"

"Well, I'm studying Spanish, for one thing," she offered.

"Too much work!" I exclaimed. "Why even bother? Lots of Mexicans speak English, and if not, you can always gesture."

She tilted her head. "So how do you suggest I fill my time?"

"You see? The language gives it away: filling time. As though life were a chore. We select 'projects' so as not to be bored. But why not just be bored?"

"You sound like Oblomov," said Alice.

"Ob-who?"

"Oblomov. Character in a Russian novel by that name. One day he got into bed and decided never to get up. Everyone thought he was lazy, but the truth was—or this was what the author was claiming—that in reality, he could see no *reason* to get up."

"And there isn't any," I said, "unless you need to make money."

"Listen, George: this is a load of crap. You didn't retire and then get into bed. Here you are in Mexico, traveling around. Where are you going after that, do you know?"

"Italy," I told her.

"Well, that's not Oblomov, honey pie. You want to see the world."

"Not exactly," I said. "I'm not going to Italy to tour the Vatican, or see paintings by Leonardo. I'll do the same thing there that I've been doing here: just sit in cafés, read, and watch the world go by. I'm a traveling Oblomov, as it were."

"I've got it: you're a Buddhist, aren't you? All of this is an exploration of the Void, isn't it? The theory is that we stuff ourselves, we fill our lives with 'projects,' like Spanish classes, to avoid the terror of emptiness, and that we can only know reality, and ourselves, if we just stop all the busy-ness and see what happens. Am I right?"

"What's the Void?" I asked her.

She looked defeated; her shoulders slumped. "Jesus, maybe

you *are* a traveling Oblomov."

Our food came just at that moment, sparing us an uncomfortable Buddhist silence. The *pozole* was wonderful. "More alcohol?" I asked her.

She nodded. "I think I'm going to need it."

More silence, but not uncomfortable. "George, I'm sorry to ask this. Do you want to sleep with me?"

"Wow!" I countered. "Where did that come from?"

"Oh, come on," she said; "it's always in the air between a man and a woman."

"Alice, I'm twenty years older than you. I'm hardly Paul Newman, and I'm dull as a stick."

"And I'm violently turned on to you. Go figure."

"Wouldn't you rather become an Oblomovna?" I asked her. "We could both crawl into bed and do nothing together."

"Why is it that the more I hear you talk about doing nothing, the more I want to do something. In particular, fuck you silly."

"Fucking is overrated," I told her. "Dullness is where it's at."

"You're torturing me on purpose, aren't you? You're really a Zen master in disguise. You're withholding to make me crazy with desire—that's it, isn't it?"

"What is Zen?" I asked her.

"I think I may have to kill myself."

Back in my room, lying naked on my bed and looking up at the ceiling, I had to pronounce my first venture into dullness a resounding success. I mean, the idea had been to experiment with it, see where it might lead. Well, I sure found out. This was an outcome I had never imagined. I saw it as my first experiment in a series of many, although I didn't want the next encounter to necessarily be about sex. I had a powerful weapon in my hands; this much was clear. There were whole worlds out there, and I was going to conquer them. "Dullness Rules!" I thought to myself, as I drifted off to sleep.

2.

I awoke the next morning with the sun streaming through the wooden slats that hung in front of the windows of my room. Looking between them, I saw a man standing next to a burro, on which were piled colorful rugs, tied up with thin ropes. In the distance, a rooster crowed.

D.H. Lawrence was right, I said to myself; mornings in Mexico are magical. I got dressed and went back to the café in the town square, ordered a cappuccino, and looked around. Alice was nowhere to be seen, which was just as well. The conversation I wanted to have right now was with myself.

What next?, I thought. Clearly, the thing with Alice was fun, but I wanted to take it up a notch. Dullness needed greater challenges. I figured I should return to the United States, maybe go to some political rallies, stir things up. This was the time when Hillary, Bernie, and Donald Trump were criss-crossing the country, attracting huge crowds, telling them whatever it was they wanted to hear. Fertile ground for mischief-making, it seemed to me.

I checked out of the guesthouse, took a taxi to the Morelia airport, and (via Mexico City) returned to DC. Ensconced the next day in my small house in Takoma Park, I switched on my computer to see what was happening on the presidential campaign trail. I was in luck: Hillary was going to be speaking at NYU in three days. Perfect. I purchased the train tickets online, reserved a room at the Larchmont Hotel in the West Village for a week, and proceeded to make myself breakfast. This could be fun, I told myself; Hillary wasn't one to roll with the punches.

I always enjoyed staying at the Larchmont; it's very European, very low-key. Small, comfortable rooms, with the shower and bathroom down the hall. Definitely un-American: no "promotions," no commercial pitches; the place wasn't "going" anywhere. And most of the clientele seemed European, as well. A continental breakfast was served in a smallish room in the basement, which is where I found myself the next morning. I stayed a while, as people came and went, reading my tattered copy of *The Man Without Qualities* in the original German. *Gemütlich,* I thought; I could stay here forever.

But eventually I got up and walked over to Greenwich Street, to an antique watch shop I always liked to visit when I was in New York. I had purchased two or three pocket watches over the years, "real" ones like Elgins from the 1950s, that you had to wind up every day. But I didn't feel like spending money today; I just peered in the window and then made my way over to the new Whitney Museum, where I whiled away several hours until it was time for Hillary to put in an appearance at NYU.

She had a reputation for showing up at least an hour late, but I got there a bit early anyway. I figured I would wander around, try to catch the mood of the crowd. How to describe it? A bit nervous, edgy. These were, after all, Democrats, and the last time around they had high hopes that were bitterly disappointed. And yet—fools that they were—they kept striving, kept longing, kept hoping that the *next* nominee was somehow going to be different, going to fix things. What they needed, quite clearly, was a huge dose of dullness.

I turned to the guy sitting next to me. He was about thirty-five, kind of pudgy, wearing jeans, a (very) faded AC/DC T-shirt, and a Yankees baseball cap. Was he raw material for the Dullness Institute?, I wondered.

"Hi," I said, extending my hand. "I'm Bob." He shook my hand, told me he was Trevor. "A lot of people here with high hopes," I offered. "Reminds me of the Obama rallies of 2008." I looked at him sideways, cautiously. Trevor shrugged.

"He was an unknown quantity, when you think about it. We were all so eager to be done with Bush, I think anyone with a liberal vibe would have fit the bill. Hillary's very different. Her track record is there for all to see."

I grunted. "But what if, in eight years, it's the same old story? What then? Everyone here seems to be *striving,* trying to find something better. What if it doesn't exist?"

"So we should just give up?"

"Why not? By all accounts, the American Dream is finished. You're young, and even within your lifetime the US has gone downhill dramatically. Nothing is forever, after all. If you're in a losing poker game, sooner or later the smart thing is to cash in your chips, no?"

Trevor had a semi-agonized look on his face. Clearly, he wanted to believe in Hillary, and clearly, what I just said struck home. He tried to reply, but nothing came out.

"I mean," I continued, "what can *any* of these candidates do about the situation, really? They aren't magicians. Wouldn't it make sense for everyone here to just go home, and leave Hillary speaking to an empty room?"

Trevor gave me a quizzical look. "Well, *you're* still here," he said with a challenge in his voice. "You're not exactly taking your own advice."

"You're right, my man. I just want to ask her a few questions, though I can't imagine she'll be giving any of us unscripted answers. Do *you* have any questions for her, yourself?"

"Well, I was in the Occupy Wall Street movement a few years ago, and when that fizzled out, I wondered if there was any way to stop the 1 percent from destroying the country and the planet. I guess that's what I'd like to ask her."

"You are aware that she and Bill have amassed $2 billion, right? She's part of the 1 percent; those are her friends. She doesn't hang out with folks like you and me. Maybe it's time for *all* of us to throw in the towel."

This time, to his credit, he smiled. "Well, I hope you get to ask her about that," he said. At this point, with great fanfare, Hillary arrived, nearly an hour late. She climbed up to the lectern and turned a plastic face to the crowd. Was I the only one who found her grotesque?

"The White House in 2016!" she cried. The audience cheered. "American working families need a better break, and when I'm president they are going to get it!" More cheering. She proceeded to deliver what I imagined was her standard campaign trail stump speech, and I couldn't help wondering how many people there were hoping against hope. Finally, she wound it up, adding: "Let's have some questions!"

I shot my arm up. "Yes, you in the front," she said. I stood up.

"Mrs. Clinton, I admired your decision, just a few years back, to resign your position as Secretary of State. After all, all that striving, all that effort, and for what? Why, then, are you striving once again? The United States is fading, both at home and abroad, so why are you bothering with all this? You surely don't believe the foolish slogan of Donald Trump, that we can make America great again, do you?"

Before she could reply, I turned around and faced the audience. "What can *any* candidate do for us at this point in

American history? Does anyone here really believe Hillary can turn things around? Shouldn't we all just stop wishing and striving, and go home instead?"

At this point all hell broke loose. Of course, many members of the audience were enraged, but my words had apparently struck a nerve among many others. "He's right!" one woman at the back of the hall shouted. "Hillary can't do shit!" Hillary, meanwhile, was banging on the lectern, trying to get the situation under control; but it was far too late for that. The Hillary-is-useless faction began to desert in droves, until something like fifty people were left in the auditorium. And then, recorded on YouTube for the whole world to see, as most of you undoubtedly remember, was a full-blown Hillary meltdown.

"You!" she shrieked, pointing at me. "You—" Her face swelled to twice its normal size, and turned purple. She was now rolling around on the stage, apparently rabid. I turned to Trevor. "Time to hit the road, amigo." Before security could arrest us, we fled the auditorium, and melted into the large crowd of deserters outside. Half an hour later, we were sitting in a bar off Washington Square.

"Jesus," he said to me, with newfound respect, "that was quite a scene you pulled back there."

"Yeah, turned out a lot better than I imagined. I guess Hillary won't be taking the oath of office in 2017."

Trevor guffawed. "You may single-handedly be responsible for the election of Trump to the presidency." He shook his head. "You're hell on wheels, man, you know that?"

I changed the subject. "Listen, Trev: you mentioned your involvement with the Occupy Movement. I know it's pretty much a dead letter these days, but are they still holding rallies or meetings at this point? I think I'd like to pay them a visit."

He guffawed again. "What's your politics, Bob? I mean, really. What's your game?"

"It's George, actually. Here." I slid a Dullness Institute brochure across the table. "Care to join? We're looking for a few good men."

3.

Three days later I received an e-mail message from Alice. Apparently somehow, amidst the slosh of margaritas, she had conned my e-mail address out of me.

Dear George:

Does anyone besides me know who you are? Speculation is rife about the guy who put Hillary in Bellevue for a week, on a Haldol drip. Now I'm *really* sorry I didn't get to sleep with you: if there's one guy in this world who isn't dull, it's you, George. Anyway, all sex aside, I don't want this friendship—or whatever it was we had, for one day—to end. I don't know who you really are, or how much of that story you told me was true, but if the Dullness Institute is actually a going concern (empty web site, for the time being), I'd like to become a member. Hillary is a moron, and got what she deserved. Do you really live in DC? Can I come visit you? I promise to keep my hands to myself.

Fondly,

Alice Connors

Dear Alice:

I live in Takoma Park, Maryland. I was never a car salesman, and I am not wealthy. I had a career as a professor of German lit at GW. I was never married, but I did love two women very much. They both left me, one because of cancer. C'est la vie.

I am, however, really committed to the notion of dullness as a creative force—clearly on display at NYU, imo—and everything I said about being turned off by the "performance" aspect of American culture is true. As a result of that evening at NYU, I made my first convert to the cause, a fellow named Trevor Jones. He lives in NY, but we plan to get together in the future to plot the strategy of the Institute. I would love it if you were to become the 2nd convert to the cause. I suggest you visit me at a time when Trevor is free to come down (he works as a computer programmer), and we can spend a few days hashing things out.

With kind regards,

George Haskel

Dear George:

Just let me know when Trevor is coming to DC, and I'll make arrangements accordingly.

-ac

Wow, I thought; things are moving really fast. Before I write Trevor, I need to hammer out a Mission Statement. Obviously, the purpose of the Dullness Institute couldn't simply be mischief-making, or getting women sexually aroused by using reverse psychology. The encounter with Hillary and her minions actually had deep philosophical roots: to puncture phoniness and pretension; to wake people up to reality; to radically alter American culture, person by person (or crowd by crowd); and finally, to teach people that if you can learn to sit with emptiness, remarkable things can happen. This is what I wrote:

Mission Statement of the Dullness Institute

by George Haskel

Goethe wrote that "when a man strives, he errs." When I look around the United States today, most of what I see is striving, hustling. No one feels free to be truly themselves; instead, it's all selling, angling, manipulating. The result is an enormous strain in the American soul (what's left of it). Very few of us have any peace of mind, any real satisfaction in our lives. Psychologically speaking, it's a form of slavery.

All of this is the misery of what is called the American Dream, which is really the American Nightmare. In order to tolerate this way of life, we sedate ourselves with drugs, alcohol, television, cell phones, and even more posturing and manipulation, creating a vicious circle from which we can never escape. Millions want to stop living like hamsters on a wheel, but don't know how to do it. The purpose of the Dullness Institute is to teach them how; in a word, to give them back their lives.

What we are "selling," in short, is authenticity. Most Americans are living in despair; at the Dullness Institute, we seek to replace that with integrity, with genuine happiness as opposed to substitute satisfaction. While this will do wonders for the individual, the repercussions are clearly political, because the corporations that run this country make their billions off of our misery. Think of the money they rake in from tranquilizers, advertising, and electronic toys, just for starters. Think of how they, and the government, keep us in line with the carrot-and-stick psychology of hustling, striving, "progress," getting ahead. Think of the billions garnered by the sex industry, the gun industry, and the crack cocaine industry. And think what the rage and pain we suffer as a result lead to: a massacre a day at home, and the endless waging of meaningless wars abroad. When you can't stand to be in your own skin, you start killing other people.

And what has all this frenetic activity cost us, in human terms? America is a nation with very little friendship, or community, or empathy, or simple satisfaction with work. Our homicide rate, as well as our divorce rate, is the highest in the world. Hustling and self-promotion have made us the loneliest, most callous, and most bitter people on the planet. Karma, they call it: you reap what you sow.

None of this can be changed by electing any particular candidate to office, and the left-wing promise of revolution or radical social change will not, even if successful, be able to address these concerns. (Have you noticed that very few "progressives" are big on I-Thou relationships?) For striving and inauthenticity, dishonesty and manipulation, are hardly the exclusive province of any one particular party or political faction. There is, in short, no politics that promotes *non-doing*: solitude, quiet, creativity, genuine communication, and the exploration of the soul. We have grouped these behaviors under the title of "dullness," but the fact is that this is a misnomer: they are anything but dull. But they require a rejection of the frenetic life—what appears to be exciting but is actually empty and boring. We can know reality only if we stop filling our lives with crap, with noise and distraction, and instead embrace the terror of loneliness, of empty space, and of (apparent) dullness. Only then will we learn how remarkable our lives can truly be.

What, then, is our political strategy, if it is not that of electoral politics or of fomenting revolution? It has several aspects to it. The first line of action is education: teaching people about the nature of substitute satisfaction, and how (for example) their cell phones and electronic gadgets are destroying their lives. The second is public disruption, along the lines of Dada, or Surrealism, or the Situationists, as was attempted in years past, the idea being to puncture balloons, violate ossified norms and forms. (Hillary Clinton, for example, prior to her meltdown at NYU, was a balloon filled with hot air, and she was hardly unique.) And the third line of action is to radically alter American culture, person by person and group by group, so that Americans may finally live their true lives, and not someone else's idea of what their lives should be.

Is this utopian? Undoubtedly. Will it attract many people? Not at first. What we at the Dullness Institute are counting on is that reality, the joy of living one's own life, is irresistible, and thus that it will spread, like a positive epidemic. Americans may come to see that dullness leads to something revelatory—a kind of fruitful nihilism, as it were. One does not, à la Aldous Huxley, need psychedelic drugs to open the doors of perception; one only needs dullness, properly understood and cultivated.

* * * * *

In keeping with the Institute philosophy, I was practically stoned by the time I typed the last line; and not bothering to edit the text, I sent it to Alice and Trevor as an e-mail attachment with a four-word message: "What do you think?" Both of them replied within the hour. "I'm in!" wrote Trevor. Alice was equally direct: "If I don't get to sleep with you before I die, I'll kill myself." "Very funny," I wrote back. To Trevor I said: "When can you get time off from work to come down here and meet with me and Alice?" "Week after next," he replied two minutes later. The Dullness Institute was off and running.

4.

Two weeks later, two hours apart, Alice and Trevor arrived at National Airport (I refuse to use the word "Reagan" because he represents everything the Dullness Institute is opposed to). I put Alice in the guest room; Trevor agreed to sleep on the couch in the living room. Given his work schedule, we had four days to hammer out a general plan of action, plus organize our next move. We decided to kick things off with a freewheeling brainstorming session that evening, for which I bought two bottles of cold champagne and ordered a large amount of Indian takeout. The ideas flew thick and fast, along with the pappadams and the mango chutney. Alice waded right in.

"Obviously," she said, "what we need are numbers. Three today, thirty tomorrow, 3 million a year from now. I suggest we run an ad in the *New York Times*." She handed Trevor and myself a prepared copy. It read as follows:

WERE YOU PRESENT AT NYU ON SEPTEMBER 4TH WHEN HILLARY FLIPPED OUT?

WOULD YOU LIKE TO CAUSE SIMILAR INCIDENTS?

"I like it," said Trevor. "It has a certain understated insanity."

"Trev," I said, "those three lines in the *Times* are going to cost us ten grand. Ditto, a thirty-second ad on national TV. I'm willing to spring for it; the problem is that one single ad won't work. I'm told that in the ad business, it's repetition that counts. We need a whole media campaign, and that I definitely can't afford."

"The thing is," said Alice, "the Hillary meltdown is still in the news. She only recently got out of Bellevue, and is hiding out on Long Island because when she goes outside, people point and laugh. Small children throw pebbles at her. And that YouTube tape has had something like 2 million hits by now. We need to capitalize on this, and fairly quickly, before the issue goes cold. Now is the time to put the DI on the map." (It was from this point on that the Dullness Institute unofficially became known as "the DI.")

"Well, money is always the issue in politics," I said. "I suppose we could charge a membership fee for joining the DI, but as we would need at least a million for an advertising budget, we'd have to charge a fair amount, and that would prevent many people from joining. We may be screwed here."

The three of us sat there silently for a while, munching on our lamb biryani and chicken tikka masala. Alice spooned some raita onto her plate. "I still think the ad is a good idea," she finally said. "But we also need some face-to-face political organizing as well. Your dullness is very charismatic, George, as I'm sure you know."

"Well..." I began, but Trevor interrupted. "George, remember you asked me if the Occupy movement was still holding meetings? Why don't the three of us go to some of those? They might be fertile grounds for recruitment. Also, Colton Farnsworth regularly gives his 'we're on the verge of revolution' stump speech across the country; why not go and pull a Hillary on him?"

"Who's Colton Farnsworth?" asked Alice, pouring herself another glass of champagne.

"Kind of a sad case," I told her. "He's a writer who was so desperate for revolution to happen, that he slipped over the edge into fantasy and started preaching that it was inevitable, and was going to happen soon. He's turned into a kind of Pied Piper figure, especially for those who think much more with their hearts than with their heads. No shortage of those, I'm afraid."

"He sounds demented," said Alice.

"More like a schlemiel," I said, "and he has very little by way of a sense of humor, although he does have a rather large fan base. Young people in particular want to believe what he's saying."

The conversation continued into the night. We tossed a lot more ideas around, including hiring a plane to fly over New York with a banner that read, HILLARY WAS JUST THE BE-GINNING. Finally, I suggested we turn in and continue the discussion in the morning. (Trevor had already fallen asleep in his chair.) I conked out almost immediately.

At around 7 A.M., Alice crept into my room and climbed into bed next to me. "I just want to hold you, George," she whispered; "no hanky-panky, I promise." So we held each other, and it was very chaste, although I did wind up with a semi-hardon.

5.

Things moved swiftly during the next four days. Trevor offered to set up a web site, post the Mission Statement on it, and run off a thousand copies of the brochure. It turned out that the company he worked for didn't object to employees using its time or equipment for personal projects, so long as they got their company work done quickly and efficiently. And they trusted Trev; he had been with them for twelve years, and working steadily and quietly had made millions for them during that time.

Alice volunteered to be the DI secretary. This meant that mail sent to the DI would be addressed to alice@dullnessinstitute. org, and that she would field phone calls as well. Her picture would be on the web site (along with mine and Trevor's, plus short bios), and she would act as the public face of the organization. (Shortly after the site went up, Alice started receiving marriage proposals at the rate of about three a week. "Is this making you jealous, George?" I kissed the top of her head in response.)

We also decided to run Alice's ad in the *New York Times*. I agreed to cough up the ten thousand dollars this one time. Finally, we addressed the question of free publicity. Once again, Alice took the lead.

"George, since the *Times* ad is necessarily a one-shot deal, we need to find some way to get the DI in the news. The best publicity, of course, is TV. What we need is to get you on the Bill Maher show, or some equivalent of that." I rolled my eyes.

"Alice, Bill Maher isn't going to give air time to some elderly fruitcake from Takoma Park going on about authenticity versus substitute satisfaction. Besides, I'd just come off sounding like a New Age guru, and since the media is not into matters of substance, I would become the focus of their attention, which is the last thing we need. You know as well as I that the cult of personality is just more hustling."

"But we do need publicity, George," Trevor broke in. "Otherwise, the DI will never get off the ground. If we proceed with this thing, people are going to love you and hate you. They are going to project all their fantasies onto you. There's no avoiding it, and there won't be much you can do about it.

"Let me tell you something. When you made your pitch to me about dullness at NYU, there was a moment when I was hovering between two worlds, and could have gone either way. Something within me knew you were right, and wanted to go along with you. But there was another part that was afraid of you, and wanted to recoil from you, attack you. By a slim margin—and I don't know exactly why—the first part won out, and now here I am, constructing web sites and printing brochures. My point is that given our message, it's inevitable that we are going to evoke strong, irrational emotions, both pro and con.

"I had a professor in college, this was in a psychology course I was taking, who had a concept he called 'existential strain.' I think the idea originally came from George Steiner. Anyway, my prof said that certain figures, and certain concepts, evoked the feeling that we could and should be larger than what we were. Steiner's best example was Jesus Christ, who got crucified for his efforts. Another, said my prof, was Wilhelm Reich, who was metaphorically crucified by the US government. You may not see it, George, but you are doing something similar; all this stuff about living one's true life is very threatening. I'm telling you, George: watch your back. People want it and they also fear it, often with equal intensity. Don't get me wrong; I'm definitely on board. But don't kid yourself that it's going to be an easy ride. We need visibility in order for this thing to work, but it will come with a price. Especially for you."

Alice and I sat there stunned, taking it all in. This was no ordinary computer geek we had here; where did all this come from? Who *was* this guy? We were silent for a rather long time.

"Trev," I finally said, "I can't thank you enough for being honest with me, and with Alice, about the ambivalence you initially felt upon meeting me. And also for the advice you just gave me, that given enough visibility, the DI might precipitate a riot, and that I'd better be prepared for it. I'm sure you're right. I guess I'm just a bit scared, is all. Although let's face it: getting onto the Bill Maher show is rather a long shot, as far as I can see."

Silence, again. All of a sudden, the ticking of the grandfather clock standing in the foyer became very loud. Finally Alice spoke. "I guess being authentic with each other is a prerequisite for running an institute designed to promote authenticity. Trev, I should tell you that I'm in love with George." She turned to me. "Oh, I know, George, you think it's just some sort of adolescent schoolgirl crush, but it's not." She turned back to Trevor. "As in your case, he just reached in and touched me where I live, without so much as a howdya do. He talked about the tediousness of American society, how everyone was hustling, trying to impress, and trying to fill empty space so they wouldn't be bored, or terrified—exactly why I left the US and moved down to Mexico. He sounded like a natural Buddhist—someone who knew the doctrine without ever having studied it. I realized that all the guys I had been involved with were classic American hustlers, who had absolutely no idea who they were, or what they were. And I thought, this guy is the real McCoy, and I felt I had to have him in my life."

Trevor smiled. "Well, obviously I didn't know the specifics, but I had a feeling something like that was going on. Good for you, Alice."

"So," he continued, looking at me now, "what's *your* Achilles' heel, George?"

"Oh, that's pretty easy," I replied; "I'm lonely."

The two of them stared at me. "That's it?" said Alice. "This whole project was conceived because some retired German lit professor happened to be lonely?"

"Is that so strange? The conversation we've just been having, are having right now: How many people in your life could you have this with? With how many have you had anything like this in the last five years, maybe even ten?"

"None," she admitted.

"Trev?"

"Nada. Big fat zero."

"So I guess the personal *is* political," I said. "We have no one to talk to, but it's hardly because we're psychotic. No one in this tragic country has anyone to talk to, not really, and that's not an accident. So yes, I want to turn the culture upside down, but I also want intimacy in my life. It's finally not much more complicated than that. I'm lonely, and I'm tired of being lonely. End of story."

Something broke after that; the three of us found it much easier to be together. We hung out all day, tossing ideas back and forth. And that night, Alice and I did more than cuddle.

6.

We spent the next three days working on DI development, having long lunches in cafés off Dupont Circle, cruising the Smithsonian, the Phillips Collection, and the National Gallery of Art, laughing hysterically at politically incorrect jokes, and in general being the three happiest people on earth. Alice announced that she would return to Morelia, rent out her house, and move to Takoma Park; Trev planned to ask his boss if he could work four days a week, ten hours a day, which would mean that he could spend long weekends with the two of us, sleeping in the guest room and doing Institute work. It was as though a miracle had touched our lives; and looking back, I guess it had.

"Tell me about your girlfriends," said Alice one afternoon, after we had finished making love.

"Jesus, woman, your sense of timing isn't exactly the best." She laughed.

"No, George, I really want to know. Start with the one who didn't have cancer."

I sighed. "It was a mirage," I said, "though it took me a couple of years to figure it out. Irene was afraid of being close to anyone, even on a friendly basis. I guess she had been hurt a lot, I don't know. Or maybe she was just wired up that way. It was as though she were living in a glass gazebo. But I was wet behind the ears; I didn't have the psychological savvy of our friend Trevor, and I didn't get it, that her unavailability was the source of the attraction. I fucked her brains out, but it didn't matter: her soul was somewhere else. So it was easy for her to leave me, after two years of being together, but it was devastating for me. It just took me some time to understand that what I had had was a nonrelationship."

"God, that sounds awful," said Alice. "'Looking for love in all the wrong places.' I guess that could be the theme song of the DI." She paused for a moment. "And the one who had cancer?"

"Ten years. Definitely left me an atheist. I'd prefer to talk about it some other time."

We lay in bed for a long while after that, not saying anything. Finally Alice turned to me. "I'm not going to leave you, George. I want you to know that." Another pause. "Is there anything you want to know about my past loves?" she asked.

I stroked her hair. "No, my dear. It doesn't really matter. Let's be here now, as the hippies used to say."

7.

We still had to plan our next political event. We finally decided to attend a Colton Farnsworth lecture, see what we could stir up, or whom we could bring over to our side. It was being held on the Homewood Campus of Johns Hopkins University in Baltimore, and Trev was in for the weekend. The three of us drove up in my car, and I parked a few blocks from campus, at 30th and North Calvert Streets, in a kind of dull, lackluster neighborhood. Our strategy was to place ourselves at different points in the audience, and then chime in as though we were independent voices. Our own brand of hustling, I suppose.

It turned out that there was an entrance fee at the gate, fifteen dollars a head. If Colton was right about revolution being imminent, it was apparently going to come from folks with enough disposable income to pay top dollar for forty-five minutes of talk. The three of us paid the fee, then fanned out into the audience, which probably numbered about five hundred people. They were casually dressed; no one looked especially poor. I wondered how many ex-Occupiers were in the crowd.

When Colton finally arrived, I did a doubletake: he was a dead ringer for Trotsky. Medium height and build, goatee, wire-rimmed glasses—it seemed like a parody. Someone from the Johns Hopkins Student Association introduced him as "the most critical voice in America today," and Colton stepped up to the lectern.

"We live in revolutionary times," he began. "Occupy Wall Street put its finger on the problem, that 1 percent of the population controls most of the wealth and is oppressing the remaining 99 percent. The situation is one of neofeudalism, and unless we rise up against our masters, against corporate fascism, we are doomed. But resistance is forming, across the country. Americans are increasingly aware of what is going on, and they are moving to take matters into their own hands."

Colton went on in this vein for nearly an hour. The whole speech was a fairy tale, a description of a country that didn't exist, except in his own mind. In addition, it was actually quite boring. The delivery was often monotonic; it was obvious that he had given this talk many times over. But it was equally clear that he was preaching to the converted, to people who, like himself, needed the fairy tale in their lives in order to function. Like him, they had stuffed the hole in the soul with "revolution." Getting them off the drug in favor of tolerating the Great Unknown was definitely going to be a hard sell.

"Of course, there are no guarantees we shall succeed," he cried, "but that doesn't really matter. It's the *gesture* that counts. We must fight fascism because it is evil, and we must fight all the evils of the world all of the time!" The crowd rose to its feet in a standing ovation, applauding wildly. When the noise subsided, Colton asked if there were any questions.

"How long before the masses rise up, do you think, Mr. Farnsworth?"—this from a woman of about twenty-five, on the right side of the auditorium. Colton nodded vigorously. "No one can be sure, of course, but I would guess two to three years at the outside." At this point Alice caught his eye. "Woman in the back," he called out.

"I'm curious about your picture of the US as being at some sort of revolutionary crossroads," she said. "Soup kitchens and tent cities fly the American flag above them, and recent polls make it clear that most of the population doesn't resent the top 1 percent at all. They just want to join them. And where is the Occupy movement now? It had *no* mass support among the American people, isn't that so? It seems to me that this 'revolutionary moment' of yours is a fantasy."

Colton was a bit taken aback, but was nevertheless undaunted. "It's true that many Americans identify with their oppressors rather than resent them," he said; "it makes their lives easier, after all. But it is not likely that this state of affairs can continue much longer. I would venture to say—"

Alice interrupted him. "62 percent of the American public approve of drone strikes against innocent civilians," she shouted. "More than 50 percent approve of torture." Closing in for the kill, Trevor suddenly spoke up, from the opposite side of the room.

"A revolution requires guns, arsenals, and these are being stockpiled by the right, not the left. Do *you* have an arsenal, Mr. Farnsworth? Do you even own a gun?"

"Well, no, I—" It was my turn.

"So other people are going to put their lives on the line for your imagined revolution, but not you yourself? What exactly is your role in this bloody drama?" By now Colton was red in the face.

"Listen!" he fairly yelled. "Someone has to create the ideology that makes the revolution possible. Writing, reporting, analyzing, lecturing—this is my unique role in all this."

"Where is Colton's Colt .45?" cried Alice. Everybody

laughed. To his credit, Colton didn't turn purple and roll around on the stage, like Hillary, but he had clearly lost the audience. Someone else spoke up, a man in his early sixties, who looked a bit like a college professor, with a slender build, salt-and-pepper hair, and tortoise-shell glasses.

"Mr. Farnsworth," he said, "I've written several books on socialist revolution. They require certain conditions in order to take off and succeed, and these conditions do not obtain in contemporary America—not even slightly. I'm sorry to tell you this, but you are living in a dream world."

Trevor, now, shouting: "How about we all go out for a beer?" And with that, people began to drift out of the auditorium, and onto North Charles Street, in search of bars (or, perhaps, cars). I went up to Colton and handed him a DI brochure. "You've gotta walk your talk, Colton," I told him; "otherwise you're just full of hot air, no better than Hillary, really." Colton, the poor shmuck, looked rather wilted, now more like Kerensky than Trotsky. The "revolution," apparently, was over.

I went up to the man who had spoken about socialist revolution. "Will you come with me?" I asked him; "I need to talk with you." Out on the street, I found Alice and Trevor. "This is—" The man rescued me. "Martin Green," he said. We all shook hands.

"Martin, will you come with us for a moment? We need to distribute some pamphlets." We all walked back to the car, gathered up a few piles of DI brochures, and then walked the two blocks back to Charles Street.

"What now?" asked Trevor.

"Let's just go from bar to bar and hand these out. We're bound to catch some of the people who attended the lecture." Martin put his hand on my shoulder.

"You're the guy who brought down Hillary!" he exclaimed.

"I recognize you from the YouTube clip. And now you've polished off Colton Farnsworth! This was a set-up, wasn't it? Good show!" I handed him a pile of brochures, and the four of us went back to Hopkins, distributing the literature to passersby along the way. "Join us!" we cried, as we handed out the pamphlets. "Colton Farnsworth is yesterday's news. Call us!" As it turned out, a few other people recognized me from the YouTube clip, and called out, "Hey, you pulled a Hillary tonight, didn't you!" "Join us!" I replied, and handed out more brochures.

The four of us finally returned to the car. "Do you need a ride?" I asked Green. "If you don't mind," he replied, "though I live in Northwest Baltimore" (he pronounced it "Balmer"). "So you're Jewish," I winked. He laughed. "Good call," he said.

"Hey, one quick question: Can you get out to Takoma Park tomorrow? The three of us would really like to talk to you." I handed him my card, with the address printed on it. "Take a taxi, if you want; we'll reimburse you. Lunch at noon, OK?"

"Sure," he replied; "I haven't had this much fun in years." We dropped him off at his house, and then I drove around the corner and parked the car. "Well, muchachos, what do you think?"

The debriefing went on for about an hour. Alice declared that she thought Green was first-rate. "He delivered the killer punch, didn't he?" she said. "The coup de grâce. The more so since he is such a gentle guy, very soft-spoken."

"Yeah," put in Trevor; "ol' Colton was pretty much fried after that, along with your Colt .45 remark. I hope Martin comes tomorrow—we could use someone like him on the team. He has the requisite streak of frivolity, I think."

And the rest, as they say, is history. Martin did show up the next day, and I made salad and eggplant parmigiana, which we washed down with Chianti. "Trevor thinks you have a streak of frivolity, Martin. Would you agree?"

"Well," he said, his face flushed with wine, "I'm a believer in *serious frivolity*. I do not, however, endorse frivolous seriousness."

"Good man," I said. "So you'll join the team? We could use an historian-cum-political scientist. I take it you've read the brochure, so you know what we're up to."

"Oh, I loved it. Agreed with every word. I just don't know how you are going to translate it into a political movement. I mean, you yourself say that your heritage is Dada and the Surrealists and so on. Any person or group who is going to talk about the authentic life is going to be marginalized, at best. Most people don't want the authentic life. You know that, right? Dostoyevsky nailed that in *Karamazov,* and Plato a couple of millennia before that. Most people want the shadows, not the light. And I know that unlike our friend Colton Farnsworth—a well-meaning putz, but a putz nonetheless— you are not into symbolic gestures. So what are we really talking about?"

"We are talking, Mein Herr, about serious frivolity. I honestly believe most people *do* want the authentic life; they just don't know how to go about getting it. That's where we come in. Our numbers will grow, and as they do we will be able to formulate strategies for how to assist them. I *know* it's utopian. I *know* it sounds like Charles Fourier. But capitalism blows dogs, and socialism ain't a whole lot better. Can you see a rigid, humorless turkey like Colton Farnsworth as head of state? God help us! So we need to develop a program of pragmatic utopianism, and I'm sure you can contribute to this. What do you actually do, by the way?"

Green smiled. "I'm an itinerant academic," he said. "Mostly I write, but I also get the occasional visiting university appointment. However, I'm not hurting for cash, because about ten years ago I accidentally wrote a best-selling novel—forty-two weeks on the *New York Times* best-seller list. Hence the house in Northwest Baltimore. You don't have to reimburse me for my taxi fare, by the way." He winked.

"What was the name of the book? Maybe we've heard of it."

"*Stalin Can Kiss My Tuchus.*" The three of us burst out laughing. "Oh surely not," I countered.

"I read it," said Trevor. "A work of genius. Sort of like the comical version of *Darkness at Noon.*"

"Jesus," I said, "hard to make a comedy out of that one. Anyway, look at us: we now have a computer programmer/psychologist, an attorney, an historian, and—most important of all—an ex-German lit professor. Nothing can stop us now. A toast!" I cried: "To the Dullness Institute. May it convert the world, from misery to joy!"

"Hear, hear!" We all raised our glasses. "You're in Martin, yes?" "Sure, why not, Mein Schatz," he grinned; "I'm definitely in."

The next week was a busy one for Alice: no less than thirty calls and e-mails in response to our brochure. It was fun eavesdropping on her conversations.

"Oh, socialism is nowhere," she informed one caller. "The only real difference between it and capitalism is a fairer distribution of wealth. Which is fine, I'm in favor of that. But spiritually speaking, it's pretty much the same idea: money, power, expansion, and substitute satisfaction. And did you see how grim Colton Farnsworth is? He reminds me of an old sixties saying, 'If I can't dance I don't want to be part of your revolution.' The guy means well, but let's face it: he's a douche bag."

When she hung up I said to her: "Douche bag? You're starting to sound like me." "That's good!" she retorted.

Meanwhile, The Four Horsemen of the Apocalypse, as we began to refer to ourselves, planned two projects for the DI:

1. A meeting of the thirty-odd callers who declared an interest in the DI, to be held on the front lawn of my house two Sundays from then;

2. Figuring out how to get me on the Bill Maher show.

"Alice," I said, "you're a genius." "I agree," she replied, "but are you referring to anything in particular?"

"Indeed," I told her. "A while back—it seems like ten years ago, now—you declared: 'three today, thirty tomorrow, 3 million next year.' Well, we're already at Stage 2. The sky's the limit."

"Hey," she said, "thinking big is what made this country great, right?" She stuck out her tongue.

8.

A sunny Maryland afternoon in October. In front of my house, the Four Horsemen. Fanning out across the lawn, twenty-eight people, ages twenty to fifty, give or take, in search of the authentic life. Martin had sprung for wine, beer, and chips. The mood was festive.

"Hillary's a douche bag!" someone yelled. Alice stepped forward. "George has informed me that that's become my favorite expression. But yes, there's no question about it: Hillary's a douche bag. The question is how to turn this insight into a political movement." Everyone laughed.

"And I think I know how," she went on. "How many of you have seen *30Rock*?" Most of the hands went up. "Well," she continued, "I'm a big fan of Tina Fey's, and on one of those shows she said, 'I will not tolerate douchebaggery.' This is an important tenet of the DI. Most of our lives in the US boil down to little more than douchebaggery, as you well know. We at the DI are here not only to reject it, but to create lives for people that are meaningful; that are 100 percent douchebag-free. And right now, this activity is precisely the most meaningful life any of us can have. On that note, let me turn you over to George."

"Thank you, Alice. As some of you know, I was a professor of German literature at GW. In fact, I spoke German before I spoke English. In any case, one of my favorite writers is Nietzsche, and one of my favorite quotes from Nietzsche is from his book *Human, All Too Human.* Here it is:

'The best way of beginning each day well is to think on awakening whether one cannot this day give pleasure to at any rate one person. If this could count as a substitute for the religious practice of prayer, then this substitution would be to the benefit of one's fellow men.'

"This is the goal of the DI, and I want to stress that it is a *political* goal. It is possible, at some early point, that capitalism made people happy. And perhaps, at one time, socialism did as well. But those days are over. The time has come to try something new. The four of us, and all of you here, are the founding members of this movement, the attempt to try something new, and to pass it on to other people. You've read the Mission Statement; you know what we are about. Today, we are going to put our heads together and plan our next moves: classes, seminars, education, publicity, strategy, political maneuvers, and how to get me on the Bill Maher show. [Laughter] This will be an open forum for discussion, and everyone's voice counts. Before we begin, I'm going to ask Alice, Trevor, and Martin to say a few words about themselves."

And so the day went. A former colleague of mine at GW, a professor of French, happened to be in Paris at the time of the May-June '68 uprising, and spent the two months in the amphitheater of the Sorbonne. There, questions were asked that are typically not allowed in mainstream society: What is man? How shall we live? How can we create a meaningful life for all our citizens? Do people have to suffer? And so on. Well, that afternoon in Takoma Park was like that; like breathing pure oxygen. By 6 P.M., most of the new DI members were weeping. And I, I wept along with them.

9.

Would you believe it, gentle reader? I made it onto the Bill Maher show. Here's how it happened. As the months went by, DI membership grew. In fact, it swelled, both by word of mouth and through the Net. In the latter category was the web site, with the Mission Statement attracting more and more people; and also the two videos on YouTube—the one of Hillary rolling on the floor, and the one of Colton Farnsworth with egg on face (metaphorically speaking). The videos went viral, until a teenage nephew of Maher's finally sent them to him, told him about the DI, and said that I was the evil mastermind behind it all. "Have him on the show," he wrote his uncle; "it'll be a blast."

I later found out that Maher wrote back, "Yeah, a blast from hell!" but he was nevertheless intrigued, to the point that Alice finally got a phone call asking if I might be available on such-and-such a date. "He's pretty busy," she told Maher's secretary, "but I'm sure he'd be delighted to spend some time talking with Mr. Maher." She put down the phone.

"George!" she screamed; "my panties are wet!"

"That's supposed to be news?" I shot back.

"No, I'm serious. Bill Maher wants you on the show, roughly two weeks from now. It's called *Real Time,* in case you didn't know. I'm gonna wait a day and call back tomorrow to confirm. OK?"

"Enough kidding around, Alice. I'm trying to read Heinrich von Kleist."

"I don't care if you're trying to read Heinrich von Wiener Schnitzel. This is not a joke."

I appeared at the door to her office. "What the hey?"

"I'm calling back tomorrow to confirm. Yes or no?" I sank into the armchair next to her desk. "Whew! What a break. This is fabulous. Only one problem: I'm no good with crowds."

"Wha? You're great with crowds."

"Not a crowd of several million."

"So just pretend you're talking to Bill; which you will be. Listen, you just need a little prep, a little rehearsing. I'll rally the troops. Trev will be down this weekend, and I'll have Martin join us. And smile! You're on candid camera!"

Quite a sense of humor my girlfriend has.

So Saturday morning we all met at the house, and Alice and Trevor whipped up a breakfast of Western omelettes and bagels. I felt like drinking Scotch, but I settled for coffee. Martin was the first to address the issue.

"What's your primary objective, in doing this interview?" he asked me.

"I have two objectives," I said, "and they are interrelated. One, to be taken seriously; two, to persuade people to join the DI and start living authentic lives. I guess a third would be to convince the audience that with a large enough participation, this could become a significant political movement."

"Tall order," interjected Trevor. "Keep in mind that he's a comedian, and very good at it. He will probably want to make you look foolish, so as to get some laughs. We need to role play this so that you've got your comebacks all lined up."

Which is what we did. We brainstormed and role played all day long, at the end of which Alice pronounced me ready. The date was set for April 8. I didn't get a whole lot of sleep in the ensuing two weeks, I have to admit.

But the day finally arrived, and I got to the studio in LA three hours ahead of time. The makeup crew dusted my face so it wouldn't reflect the glare from the lights. From the wings, I heard Bill addressing the audience.

"Our next guest is a very unlikely one, ladies and gentlemen. A former professor of German literature at George Washington University, he became widely known for the famous Hillary Clinton meltdown of last year. Let me show you the clip." At this point, Bill screened the video of my challenging Hillary, and of her going berserk. The audience had a good laugh. "And another presidential candidate bites the dust!" cried Bill. "George, come on out here. Ladies and gentlemen, George Haskel."

Mild applause. I strode across the stage, trying not to trip or puke with fear. Bill and I shook hands, and I sat down.

"So, professor, you're apparently a mischievous guy, eh?"

"Well, you know, Bill, ever since I retired, I needed to fill all that empty space, so I figured taking down Hillary was a good place to start."

Someone in the audience booed. Bill smiled. "I guess we can't make everyone happy," he shrugged. "But seriously: Why Hillary? And what is this Dullness Institute you started around that time? [Shows brochure to audience.] Frankly, you seem anything but dull."

Before I could answer, Bill said to the audience: "Hillary wasn't George's only victim, folks. He and his band of merry men—"

"And woman," I interjected.

"—right, Alice Connors, your assistant at the Institute—also took down the radical socialist writer and speaker Colton Farnsworth. Let's have a look at that clip." Everyone laughed when the video got to the part where Alice made the comment about the Colt .45. "At least Farnsworth didn't wind up in Bellevue," Bill remarked. "No seriously, George, you're obviously a bright guy, but all of this looks looney tunes. What gives?"

"Bill, it's hardly looney tunes to take the frontrunner for the Democratic nomination for president and blow her out of the water. Nor is it looney tunes to expose an influential author who is claiming that revolution is right around the corner, as someone who has gone off the deep end. The American people needed to see how empty both of these people, and both of these political positions, are; and thanks to You-Tube—and yourself, I might add—they have. None of this is looney tunes."

"Are you offering the American people an alternative, then?" he asked.

"I am, but they have to be brave enough to grasp it. It's rather difficult to summarize in just a few minutes, so I encourage anyone watching this program to go to our web site—www. dullnessinstitute.org—and read our Mission Statement."

"Isn't your goal authenticity?" Maher asked. "I don't see how that can be turned into a political movement. So in this country we are going to have Democrats, Republicans, and Authentics? Are you really serious about that?" The audience laughed.

"Bill," I said, in a kind of low voice, "I'm going to ask you not to do what you are doing. You're bigger than that. You know as well as I do that the media in this country focuses on soundbites, and reduces people and ideas to quips and formulas. It won't be hard for you, or any major media figure, to make me look like a crank. If you insist on doing that, I can't stop you. But I'm talking about real existential freedom for a lot of people, and I'd hate for that opportunity to be lost."

And for once on his show, Bill was properly cowed. He looked at me for a moment and then said, rather quietly, "So you want me to be authentic?"

"You certainly have it within you, amigo; I've seen your show many times. Under all the jokes, is a big heart." And at this point, the impossible happened: Bill got up, sat down next to me, and gave me a hug. The audience went nuts.

"George Haskel, everybody!" he cried. "George Haskel!" I got up, we shook hands, and I walked off the stage.

I stayed that night with a former colleague of mine who taught at UCLA, and lived in Westwood. No sooner did I get to his house than the phone rang. Alice, who else.

"My god, George, you really knocked the ball out of the park, didn't you? The phone has been ringing off the hook for the last hour. Thanks to you, we might actually make that 3 million membership mark."

"So you think I did OK?" I teased her.

"*OK?*" she fairly screamed. "*OK?* Oh, you're joking. Very funny. Yes, you did OK. Trevor wants to have a word with you."

"Hey George. That's it, kiddo: you're my guru. I kiss the hem of your toga, Socrates. How do you do it, George? What's your secret?"

"Trev, before you start drooling on my toga, keep in mind that it was Maher who did it. He *chose* to be authentic; I just laid the option out before him. Like I did with you at NYU 5 million years ago. You said it yourself: you could have gone either way. Well, the same applies to Maher. Like you, he's a good guy. So *he* gets the credit, not me. Let's not start a cult of personality here."

"I worship your jockstrap."

"Goodnight, Trev."

10.

In the wake of the Maher show, all hell broke loose. DI membership rose to one hundred thousand, and we had to start charging for it so we could rent another house in Takoma Park and hire a secretarial staff to work under Alice. Trev took an indefinite leave from work, sublet his place in New York, moved into my guestroom on a full-time basis, and agreed to a salary of 50 percent of what he had been earning as a programmer. Martin put $250,000 into a bank account in the name of the DI, and Alice resurrected her legal skills so as to incorporate the DI as a tax-exempt NGO. The second house, which we eventually purchased, started hosting seminars on the authentic life, with all four of us acting as instructors. No one was getting a lot of sleep.

I also started getting a fair amount of hate mail, sent to alice@theDI, but addressed to me. I called these people "trollfoons," which represented a cross between a troll and a buffoon. Many of these folks thought I was Jewish, for some reason, so "haskeldirtyjew" was a typical greeting. Occasionally I would reply, suggest that the authentic life was much more rewarding than hating someone you didn't even know, but I didn't make much headway trying to teach them that living well was the best revenge. Without exception, they would reply with more venom. "Haters gonna hate," as one of my college roommates was fond of saying, fifty years ago. These people were good examples of existential strain in action, to borrow one from Trevor.

The Four Horsemen settled down to plan our next move. Trevor got the brilliant idea of renting the movie *Gandhi*, by Richard Attenborough, for inspiration. When it came to the part where Gandhi marches to the sea and makes salt—explicitly forbidden by the British Raj—Martin cried out, "That's it!"

"What's it?" I said; "we march to the Potomac and make salt?"

"Vey iz mir, George. No. We get the one hundred thousand DI members together, march to the Potomac, and collectively throw our cell phones into the river."

"Martin, you magnificient bastard!" I exclaimed. "Yes, let's rock the digital world."

And so the notice went out to the membership that on June 1st, we would all congregate on the waterfront in Alexandria, Virginia, right near the Torpedo Factory Art Center in Old Town, and throw our cell phones into the river, while shouting "No more digital crap!" (Those without a phone were asked to buy a cheap one for the occasion.)

"*Alea iacta est!*" cried Alice. "Julius Caesar, 49 B.C.," she added. "Hey, I'm not just a pretty face."

Trevor changed the subject. "You might want to get yourself a bulletproof vest, George. Noxia and Floogle are not going to like this."

"Not to mention the Alexandria police," I added.

Things got quiet after that.

11.

I had no idea how many people would show up in Alexandria on June 1st, especially since most of the one hundred thousand DI members, I was guessing, did not live in the DC Metropolitan area. I figured, if we were very lucky, it would be about five to ten thousand, so I contacted the Alexandria chief of police, to ask if we would need a permit to assemble.

"Definitely," he told me, "and I'm not going to grant it."

"Any particular reason?" I asked him.

"Can't have thousands of people congregating out at the waterfront," he replied.

"But it often happens with tourists there, no?"

"Sure, but this is a political demonstration," he countered; "very different thing."

"Well, when you think about it, this group is pretty harmless. I'm going to make a short speech, whoever's there will toss their cell phones into the river, and then we'll leave. Not really very political, but even if it were, doesn't the First Amendment guarantee the right of lawful assembly?"

"I don't give a damn about the First Amendment, Mr. Haskel. No permit, and that's final."

"Can I quote you on that?" He hung up.

I thought that this might possibly require a change of tactics, but I wasn't sure how to go about that. In any case, I spent the next two days working on a statement of intent, which I finally posted on the DI web site, and which then got carried on many other sites as well.

June 1st

By George Haskel

As most of you know, the DI will be hosting its first group political event on this day, when many of you will come to Alexandria and congregate around the Torpedo Factory Art Center, on the waterfront. I'll make a short speech on the meaning and purpose of the event, and then those of you who wish to (hopefully, all) will throw your cell phones into the Potomac. (I don't own one myself but will buy a cheap version for the occasion.)

It turns out, however, that the Alexandria chief of police has denied our request to congregate peacefully, which is perhaps no surprise. It is also in violation of our First Amendment rights, about which, the chief informed me, "I don't give a damn." As the event is less than two weeks away, we don't have time to go to court. Hence, I suggest we show up as individuals rather than as a specific political organization; which means it would be best not to display the letters "DI" on any signs or placards. Whether that will make a difference in terms of getting arrested, I have no idea, but I'll say a few words about potential tangles with the police below. In the meantime, I see nothing wrong with carrying placards, and I would suggest slogans such as

CELL PHONES KILL

ENOUGH DIGITAL NONSENSE!

TIME TO REDEFINE "PROGRESS"

YOU ARE NOT IMPORTANT BECAUSE YOU HAVE A CELL PHONE

CELL PHONES DESTROY COMMUNITY

and so on.

What are we after? Why are we throwing these electronic devices into the water? Some of this has already been covered in the Mission Statement, but let me clarify what I think this event represents. As I wrote in the Statement, the American Dream is really a nightmare, a world of hustling, competition, and hyper-individuality, which has finally generated a huge need for substitute satisfactions so as to sedate the resulting depression and loneliness. One of the most addictive "drugs" in this category is the cell phone, which most Americans are now glued to nearly 24/7. It enables them to believe they are not alone, to feel important, to think they are part of techno-logical "progress," and to hustle better—promote themselves and their careers—as though that were the purpose of life. It is the most visible symbol of the American Dream, as well as of our failure as human beings.

This failure has many dimensions; Professor Sherry Turkle of MIT has written about it extensively. She says that the phone has effectively destroyed meaningful conversation, rendering it superficial. It has reduced our capacity for empathy, and our ability to enjoy solitude. It has made us much less creative, and much less capable of reflecting on things. Author Jonathan Franzen writes that "digital technology is capitalism in overdrive, injecting its logic of consumption and promotion, of monetization and efficiency, into every waking minute." Philip Roth adds, I cannot see how anyone can "believe he [is] continuing to live a human existence by walking about talking into a phone for half his waking life." Neither can we. The cell phone has done much to erode human values in America and elsewhere.

It is for this reason that we at the DI are promoting an event that says No to the damage wreaked on our humanity by cell phones and related technologies. By throwing them away, we make the commitment not to use them anymore, as well as the statement that they are the epitome of our cultural disease. We say to our fellow Americans: these toys are not progress, but rather stupidity.

Which will, of course, generate great animosity toward us, caused by what I like to call "existential strain." The highest goal of a human being is to search for his or her own truth, come what may. Everyone knows this, but few do it. Instead, they follow the accepted narrative of being sheep, good little boys and girls. When, as a result, they come across other people violating that narrative, and choosing instead to live authentic lives, they become enraged, because it reminds them of what they themselves could be but are afraid to be; an awareness that they mask with drugs of various sorts (including cell phones). And so they become bitter, and go on the offensive.

Why did the Nazis burn the books of Freud and Reich? Because these books were guides to finding the authentic self. Why did the police attack Occupy demonstrators with pepper spray? Because these folks reminded the cops that they were little more than compliant servants of the state—very much *un*free. Examples of this phenomenon can be multiplied indefinitely.

As a result, it is my responsibility to tell all of you to be prepared for a possible adverse reaction on the part of the Alexandria police. Do not wear jewelry or anything the police can grasp. Bring vaseline and handkerchiefs to protect yourself from tear gas. Perhaps wear a bicycle helmet. I am not trying to scare you, only to be realistic: existential strain is especially strong among the police and the military because they in particular don't follow their hearts, and when they see people who *are* doing that, it reminds them of their self-betrayal. The resulting tendency is to lash out, not against their real oppressors, but against those who are actually trying to set them free.

There is one other thing I would like to suggest as a preparatory measure in keeping with the Dada-Surrealist spirit that is part of the DI way of thinking: please bring a pastrami sandwich to the event, along with your phone. If the police should go on the attack, of course run, get out of the way— but not before you fling your sandwich at them. The attack, if it should occur, will be an expression of their insanity, and so it will be valuable for us to respond with our own brand of lunacy, in effect telling them how crazy their hyper-controlled way of life really is. We at the DI are engaged in political theater, as well as in politics.

But of course politics comes first. As Mario Savio of the Free Speech Movement said over fifty years ago,

"There is a time when the operation of the machine becomes so odious, makes you so sick at heart, that you can't take part. You can't even passively take part! And you've got to put your bodies upon the gears and upon the wheels, upon the levers, upon all the apparatus, and you've got to make it stop! And you've got to indicate to the people who run it, to the people who own it—that unless you're free, the machine will be prevented from working at all!"

Finally, to those members of the Alexandria police force who may be reading this, I wish to say to you: Defect! You don't have to spend the rest of your life in society's iron cage, hating people who want to be free and who want you to be free. Join us, and know the joy of living an authentic life.

As Edward R. Murrow used to say, Good night and good luck.

* * * * *

To my great satisfaction, this online text got reproduced, in its entirety, by a number of other web sites, such as Truthout, AlterNet, and Common Dreams. Local Virginia newspapers also gave us free publicity by reporting on the upcoming event, and quoting from my post, although most of the coverage was negative ("deluded hippies," etc.). But much to my surprise, the *Baltimore Sun* and the Annapolis *Capital Gazette* both came out with thoughtful editorials on the question of what cell phones and electronic gadgets were doing to American society, citing the critical comments of Turkle, Franzen, and Roth. The *Washington Post*, of course, maintained a stony silence.

During the last week in May, several hundred DI volunteers swung into action, plastering parts of Virginia, Maryland, and DC with flyers announcing the upcoming event. The *Sun* did an interview with me ("Wizard or Crackpot?"), giving me the opportunity to repeat the ideas presented in the post on the web site; this in turn got reprinted in the Richmond, Virginia, *Times-Dispatch*. All in all, the coverage wasn't bad.

The event was set for noon on June 1st. Martin, Trevor, Alice, and I got to Alexandria around 10 A.M.; a police contingent was already present, although (thankfully) without those dark plastic shields they often wear to emphasize their inhumanity. I had brought a megaphone and a folding chair with me. By noon there were nearly one thousand gathered on the waterfront, although I'm guessing a portion of these were curious onlookers. Some DI members had taken my suggestions for placards, but the most ubiquitous sign was the emblem of a cell phone inside a red circle, with a red slash cutting across it. I guess my favorite placard was ELECTRONIC TOYS WON'T FILL THE HOLE IN YOUR SOUL. At around noon, I unfolded my chair and stood on it, megaphone in hand.

"I want to thank all of you for coming to this important event," I began. I didn't get much further, being drowned out by a police megaphone.

"This is the Deputy Chief of Police of Alexandria. We have to ask everyone to clear the area. No permit was issued for this event, and it thus constitutes illegal trespass. If this group doesn't disperse within ten minutes, we will be obliged to arrest you." (Vans for this purpose were now parked off to the side.)

"Officer," I replied over my megaphone, "this is a public area. There is no illegal trespass going on."

"I repeat," he said, ignoring me, "you have ten minutes to clear the area."

"Since we have ten minutes," I told the crowd, "let me make a brief statement as to why we are here. Then those of you who wish to can throw your cell phones into the river, and we can all go home. We are doing this as a comment on a society that has gone horribly wrong—"

At that point the police charged into the crowd, batons swinging. They had waited all of one minute out of the promised ten. I was knocked unconscious and wound up in the Virginia Hospital Center, along with dozens of other DI protesters, who were badly beaten. The police department subsequently issued a statement that their actions had been necessary to clear the area, the more so since the demonstrators "constituted a threat to the American way of life." (He got that right, I later reflected.) All in all, a pretty bloody afternoon.

Most of the newspapers reporting the event picked up on this theme, adding phrases such as "intellectual rabble" and "misguided Luddites." (I was amazed they even knew who the Luddites were. I was also waiting for Spiro Agnew's comment about the "nattering nabobs of negativism.") But—again, to my great surprise—the *Baltimore Sun* remained in our corner, calling the event a "police riot," labeling the Alexandria police "dishonorable," affirming that the subject of technology in American society needed to get a public airing, and arguing that "the demonstrators' attempt to throw away their phones would, if allowed, have been an effective way of opening up the debate." The *Sun* also pointed out that the aborted demo was peaceful: "This demonstration would have hurt no one except the fragile egos of the Alexandria police, who foolishly chose to elevate the confrontation into a war about civilization." (Actually, not all that foolish, I thought.) Who the hell wrote this?, I wanted to know.

I issued a short statement, which did get picked up by a number of newspapers and web sites, to the effect that "I hope Americans can now see that the agenda of the Dullness Institute is extremely relevant to the question of who we are as a nation. Alternative voices are not allowed in our society. The police riot of June 1st shows how frightened some people are."

Two other events occurred in the wake of the aborted demo that served to swell the ranks of the DI even further, to something like 250,000 members. I regarded both of them as miracles, of a sort. The first was a letter to the *Washington Post* signed by Sherry Turkle, Jonathan Franzen, and Philip Roth (who in the world had arranged *this*?), calling June 1st a "day of shame...when peaceful demonstrators hoping to open up a dialogue on the impact of technology on American life got beaten up by the police." "This cannot stand," wrote the famous trio; "we demand an independent inquiry into the events of that day, and justice for those individuals who got hurt."

The second event was the courageous defection of four members of the Alexandria police department, who held a press conference denouncing the attack on the demonstrators. The leader of the group, Ted "Skip" Jackson, was quoted as saying, "I saw the Bill Maher show, where Bill decided to be authentic and embrace Mr. Haskel, and I want to say to the American public, many of whom have understandably come to fear and loathe the police, that not all of us are mindless robots. The four of us agree with Mr. Haskel's organization, that cell phones can be harmful to American society. Of course, the police need them to fight crime, but the national obsession with them, and with the social media in general, is not a healthy trend. In addition, we deplore the action taken by our colleagues, of attacking unarmed citizens who were doing nothing more than exercising their right to peaceful dissent." The "Alexandria Four," as they came to be known, were of course immediately put on administrative leave, pending further investigation; but the unprecedented defection of these truly heroic officers became national news.

The DI seemed to be getting somewhere, after all. I remember, in the wake of the 1970 shootings at Kent State University, a Gallup poll revealing that 58 percent of Americans believed that the National Guard's actions were perfectly fine, and that the unarmed students were responsible for their own deaths. Perhaps times have changed, I thought. The *New York Times* ran its own poll after the events of June 1st, and it turned out that 66 percent said that the police action had been "excessive and unwarranted," and that the protesters had the right to demonstrate.

Was light beginnng to spread, in this dark nation of ours?

12.

I was released from the hospital, recovering from a concussion, on June 4, and the four of us met on June 8 to discuss the events of June 1st and their aftermath.

"Those fools played right into our hands," exclaimed Martin enthusiastically. "As a result of their actions, DI membership has shot up, we got the endorsement of three leading thinkers and writers, four cops defected to our side, the *Baltimore Sun* sees us as heroes, and most important, the issue of our entire way of life is at long last a matter of public discussion."

"And Bill Maher wants George back on the show," added Alice. "What next? The front cover of *Time Magazine*?"

"We need to consolidate now," said Trevor, "capitalize on our gains, if you'll forgive an expression. This is actually a unique moment in American history, and it's up to us, and the DI in general, to move things forward. Our next activities are going to be very important."

I didn't say much, myself; my head still hurt. But I thought: I love these guys.

"Well, one thing," said Alice, "is that George needs to get out and lecture about it all. We received an invitation from GW, of course, but also from the Catholic University and Johns Hopkins. This is an opportunity to get the message out."

"Hopkins?" I said. "With my luck, Colton Farnsworth will show up to heckle me."

"Hey, perhaps Hillary will as well," Trevor put in. We all laughed. "So OK, George goes on the lecture circuit, preferably wearing that bandage on his head. Plus he does a few more interviews. What else? Another demo, or is it too soon for that?"

"I've got it," said Alice; "a public forum at NYU or Columbia, a one-day affair, hosting Turkle, Franzen, and Roth, along with George and Martin, to discuss the state of American culture. We need to emphasize that our beef is not just with cell phones, but with what they represent. Cell phones are only a symptom of a larger problem; they are only the far end of the hustling society—capitalism on steroids. The larger problem is that we are all living phony lives, and that some of us, at least, want to get our real lives back."

"I agree," Martin interjected; "that's exactly the ticket now, exactly the right move. A forum like that could easily draw several hundred people, and most important, continue the discussion we've started."

"OK, said Alice, "I'm on it. George, you wanna add anything?"

"My head hurts."

We left it at that.

13.

Well, Martin was right about the Alexandria police riot putting a tiger in our tank; the DI continued to grow by leaps and bounds. Plus, the one-day forum at NYU organized by Alice was a great success. Hundreds came to hear the five of us; Roth and Franzen were both wry and witty, but—along with Sherry Turkle—also very serious about their agreement with the issues that Martin and I raised, about Americans suffering from a regime of phony desires and substitute satisfactions. Nor was it just a symposium of talking heads, as there was a frequent dialogue between the five of us and the audience, reminding me of what my old colleague from the French Department had told me about the discussions at the Sorbonne in 1968. As the day was coming to a close, an attractive woman of about Trevor's age stood up to ask a question. She had long black hair and a classic oval face, with dark Sicilian eyes that were very focused, but also gentle at the same time.

"I address this to all five of you. This has been a great day, and hopefully the media will take these issues seriously and not dismiss us as hippies or utopian crackpots. My question is, How can any of this vision, launched by George Haskel and his colleagues, be implemented, be converted into reality? What steps do we have to take to become a powerful political force, such that we ultimately become irresistible? Perhaps Professor Haskel can offer the first response."

"I'm sorry," I said; "could you tell us your name?"

"Paola Marini. I'm an artist. I live in Brooklyn, and I teach at the Pratt Institute."

"Paola," I began, "when the dust settles, these questions you ask are the crucial ones for us to consider. Because the vision articulated by the Dullness Institute could well be too overwhelming for most Americans to sustain. We are calling on the greatness of the human spirit, and this is when the phenomenon of existential strain tends to get activated. The problem is that none of us at the DI see the vision as something that can be imposed on anyone; that would be a complete contradiction in terms. It would be like ordering someone to be spontaneous. For this to work as a political movement, people have to *choose* this life, have to *want* it—in effect, to want freedom more than they want security, though I hardly see the two as mutually exclusive. If we do, for example, manage to constitute ourselves as an actual political party, we have to win by attraction rather than by coercion or hustling or all of those things that characterize the Democrats and the GOP. If the DI represents a revolution of the spirit, it has to be a revolution from the ground up."

"Why does the change have to come through electoral politics?" countered Paola. "I see it more as a sea change of sensibility, brought about by millions of Americans refusing to live meaningless, inauthentic lives." [Applause]

"Well, sure; that's what I mean by a revolution from the ground up, although I don't think that necessarily precludes electoral politics. At some point, the vision has to 'go public,' so to speak, become more than just the private acts of private individuals. That's what we we're trying to do with the aborted cell phone demonstration in Alexandria. Having two major newspapers, or Bill Maher, or authors like the three writers sitting on this stage, or the four members of the Alexandria police force, come out on our side—all of these things put our vision on the map, way beyond the domain of private practice. The question you are raising, and correct me if I'm wrong, is how to take all of this to the next level."

An energetic discussion ensued, with questions and responses flying back and forth, and involving both panelists and audience. While this was going on I whispered to Martin, "We need to recruit this girl for the group, and expand from four to five. The DI could use an artist on its team." He nodded his agreement.

By then it was nearly 5 P.M., and we had to leave the auditorium. Alice stood up and addressed the crowd. "On behalf of the Dullness Institute, I want to thank NYU, our distinguished writers, and all of you, for making this day an outstanding success. Since we have to surrender the room by five o'clock, I suggest continuing this discussion in Washington Square Park, for those of you who are interested." Huge round of applause, and the audience began to disperse. I leaned across the table that the five of us were sitting at.

"Paola," I called out, "do you have a minute?" She came up to the stage. "Martin and I would love to have you on the DI team. We need an artist to illustrate our vision, if that would appeal to you, and also to help us turn that vision into reality, following up on your questions. Can we come to your studio tomorrow, and discuss it with you, maybe look at some of your work?"

Broad Italian smile. "Con piacere," she said. She handed me her card with her address on it (Williamsburg), and added, with a wink, "Non si può sbagliare." (You can't miss it).

"Allora," I said, "domani alle dieci."

14.

Martin and I arrived at Paola's place the next morning a few minutes after ten. The studio looked like a converted warehouse, and had both a work area and a living area. There were no separate rooms, just one giant space. Somehow, it was in keeping with her character. It had the definite feel of an artist's studio, with canvases leaning against the walls, and palettes and tubes of paint scattered everywhere. Paola's medium was oil, and her paintings were large and powerful. Abstract, and yet with an unmistakeable religious feel to them: the flavor of Rembrandt, or perhaps Rouault. I had never seen anything quite like it.

"Wow!" said Martin; "where did you learn to do this?"

"I studied for five years with a master in Rome. He was, in fact, very religious, but his religion came out, in his art, as pure sensuality. He often laid paint onto the canvas with a spatula. His hero was Rembrandt, and he would show me the plates of his work, like the *Portrait of Jan Six*, or *The Scholar in His Study*, and say, 'Look how the spirit hovers over his subjects, Paolina.' As the years passed, I was able to see it as well."

"But you chose to do nonrepresentational art, yourself. How did that happen?" I asked.

"Professor Haskel—"

"George, please."

"Bene, George. It was my teacher's belief that everyone is an artist of sorts, in the sense of having a particular calling. Your genius, George, is authenticity, and being able to touch people with it. Yours, Martin—I looked you up on Google—is the analysis of revolution. And mine, though I hardly think I'm a genius, is to convey the spirituality of form and color. The abstraction came naturally, spontaneously, as a kind of visceral expression. Piero's own talent was in representation, but he had no problem with my being abstract. He had such a feel for what worked and didn't work, I can't tell you. 'More orange here,' he would say, or 'these lines clash too much.' He was almost never wrong. I think that through him, I learned to love life. All true education is apprenticeship, non è vero?"

We spent the next hour looking at Paola's paintings, and then went around the corner for breakfast. I explained that Martin and I wanted her to join the DI team, but that Alice and Trevor would have to give their approval as well. We arranged for her to come down to Takoma Park the weekend after next, and offered to pay her train fare and put her up in our second house. "If you could e-mail Alice photos of some of your work beforehand, that would be great," I added.

When we finally said goodbye, Paola kissed both of us on the cheeks, European style. "Ciao, bellini!" she cried. We both laughed. Then Martin and I caught the subway to Penn Station, to get the next train back to Baltimore and DC. "Well, What did you think?" I asked him.

"Are you kidding? A young Sophia Loren. I was practically on the verge of asking her to marry me."

"Dirty old man."

"Hmph. You're one to talk."

"Good point. Seriously, she dropped in from the sky. What great artwork, eh? And she could be the poster girl for authenticity—don't tell Alice I said that."

"It's also no small thing that she's keen on translating our vision into political action," said Martin. "I really hope there are no conflicts with Alice and Trevor."

As it turned out, there weren't. Paola came down to Takoma Park ten days later, and stayed the weekend. Alice took to her right away, treating her like a younger sister. Trevor tried to hide it, but he was obviously smitten with her.

We finally agreed that Paola would come down on the weekends, as often as her schedule would allow, and stay in the second house. We'd cover her transportation costs, and provide her with a modest salary as a consultant. She would work on some paintings that captured the spirit of the DI, and also assist us in the planning of political activity.

And then, as the saying goes, there were five.

15.

I began lecturing across the United States. It was a taxing schedule, but it gave us the opportunity to make our ideas known. I even got invitations from corporations, but they had no real interest in being authentic; it was just another gimmick to them. Their goal was to use authenticity to hustle better, expand their profit margins—a "Zen for executives" kind of thing. I finally wound up declining those invitations, which was frustrating, because the money was so good.

Meanwhile, up in Brooklyn, Paola was working on a mural for the DI, tentatively called "Truth in Advertising." We got a laugh out of that. She was down almost every weekend, and eventually gave up her room in the second house and moved in with Trevor, which we all agreed was a no-brainer. Weekends were now a time for brainstorming what might be our next move, politically speaking. DI membership was actually at the half-million mark, and Martin—what would we do without him?—put another one hundred thousand in the DI bank account, to cover the costs of hiring additional staff and related expenses.

"OK, mes enfants," said Alice; "what next?"

"Can I propose a list?" offered Trevor. "Here it is. First, Paola finishes the mural and we see if we can get it prominently displayed outdoors either in New York or the DC Metro area. Second, George writes a book to go with the mural, called *Truth in Advertising*, expanding on the Mission Statement and on our plans to be a political force, at both the electoral and grass-roots level. A call to arms, more or less. Third, the rest of us need to get on the lecture circuit as well, in particular speaking to high schools. We need to create a kind of Montessori for teenagers, as it were. Fourth, we need to mount another demo or major event, so that we don't lose momentum or visibility. And finally, we could use some huge publicity boost, like George on the front cover of *Time Magazine*. [Laughter] Oh sure, you can laugh, but there was a time that getting on the Bill Maher show sounded equally quixotic. You never know."

"In terms of point number four," said Martin, "I have an idea. Do we think George could fill Madison Square Garden? It holds about eighteen thousand. I have in mind a lecture called 'What We Are Asking,' in which George lays out the goals and ideas of the DI. And we would sell tickets at two dollars a pop, so that practically anybody could attend."

"Just one thing I'd like to suggest," I put in. "I think we need to get the focus off of me, as much as possible. This movement can't be about one person, which would be a recipe for failure. It would be good if all five of us spoke, and told our personal stories—who we are, what led us to the DI, that sort of thing. Then, if you want, I could do a wrap-up along the lines of 'What We Are Asking,' and then we could have questions from the audience."

"Let me get practical, for a moment," said Alice. "Renting MSG for two hours is going to cost a bundle, and we can't afford to blow our bank account. Charging two dollars a ticket won't be enough to offset costs; we also need to go online and ask the membership for donations. Then, if and when we have the necessary cash, we can plan an event at MSG.

What's our membership count up to, by the way?"

"Over five hundred thousand now," said Martin.

"Well," said Alice, "if we could get just one dollar out of each member, that would do it. I'll start to campaign online today. We should plan the event for early January, to give us enough time to raise the money."

"Anything else?" I asked.

"Yes," said Martin. "I don't know how much of this data can be linked to the DI, but I've done a bit of research, and there's some evidence that things are changing in the US. I can't give you exact figures at this point, but here's what I've got for the period of the last two months. First, consumer spending is down. Americans are buying less, and there are a few shopping malls that are threatening to close. Second, a few more police departments besides Alexandria have experienced 'ideological resignations,' I guess you could call them. These folks have cited the Alexandria Four as their role models, and have openly stated that in their opinion, the real function of the police is not Protect & Serve, but Oppress & Intimidate. How about them apples?

"Third: the suicide rate in the military, which reached 288 among active-duty personnel in 2014, has started to decline, while at the same time the incidents of fragging—rank-and-file soldiers killing officers—has gone up.

"Holy shit," said Trevor.

"Finally," Martin concluded, "the sale of antidepressants during the last two months is down by more than 30 percent. Big Pharma is not going to be pleased."

"George, I'm definitely going to buy you that bulletproof jacket I mentioned," Trevor interjected. "You are turning into a national threat."

"It seems a tad dramatic, amigo," I replied; "the DI is still a minor player on the American scene. Anyway, thank you, Martin, for tracking on those developments, and I hope you'll keep doing it. Not that this stuff is necessarily the result of DI activity, but I'd like to cite it in my future lectures. Anything else? OK, then; let's hit it!"

The event at the Garden took place on January 6. We raised the required cash, and we nearly filled the entire space. Alice opened the forum by talking about her own experience as a teenager.

"Good evening," she began; "I'm Alice Connors, and I want to thank you all for making this event possible." She paused for a moment. "America is such a cruel place, isn't it?" [Murmurs of assent from the audience] "Let me tell you about something I participated in when I was in high school, that I'm not very proud of. There was a girl named Jane who was a bit nerdy, not part of the cool crowd. She was into chess and poetry and mathematics, while the rest of us, myself included, were into boys and nail polish and *People Magazine*. She wasn't unattractive; she just had depth, which made her a target. Now that I understand the concept of existential strain, I know what was going on: she was bigger than us. We secretly envied her, wanted what she had, but didn't know how to go about getting it; so we hated her. Retaliation took the form of not letting her sit with us in the school cafeteria; making fun of her in public, at practically every opportunity; putting a dead rat in her locker; and finally holding her down and cutting her hair, so that she looked ridiculous. Jane eventually had a nervous breakdown and transferred to another school.

"It turned out that Jane's nerdiness paid off: she's now head of the department of mathematics at one of this country's leading universities. But I'm quite sure the scars of her adolescence, of what we did to her, remain, and I bear part of the responsibility for those scars. I'm ashamed of what I did, and I would like to publicly apologize to Jane, here and now, if by any chance she is listening to this. [At this point Alice became a bit weepy, and had to fight back the tears.] The fact is, I didn't have the knowledge of why people humiliate other people. I have it now, but I didn't then; and if I had, I would have befriended Jane instead of hurting her. I would have asked her to teach me about chess and poetry and math. I would have tried to become a bigger person.

"You know, over the past few weeks I've been talking at high school assemblies in New York and the DC Metro area, and I've been telling that story. And I can see how disturbing it is to the kids in the audience, because many of them are going through something like that, either as victims or persecutors. Some of them start to cry, some run out of the room. But my message to them is that of the DI's Mission Statement: you can torture those who remind you of your own limitations, your own fears about yourself, or you can become a larger person. If you choose the former option, you may well wind up at the Pentagon, murdering innocent women and children in the Middle East with drone strikes, and taking Prozac to numb the pain. If you have the strength to choose the latter option, you too may become the target of a hate campaign. But you will be able to stand up to your persecutors, and say to them: 'You are doing this because you hate yourself. Don't do it. Let the light in, and choose authenticity instead.'

"Thank you."

The applause was deafening. I myself was moved to tears; it was the first time I had heard this story. Meanwhile, the audience began to chant: "Alice! Alice! Alice!" She started crying again, and then took a slight bow and said, "Thank you; thank you all."

Martin, Trev, and Paola then each said something about their own personal experience, and what led them to join the DI, after which I took the mike and facilitated a question-and-answer session. Finally I held up my hands.

"Could I have your attention, please? The subject of this evening's forum is 'What We Are Asking.' With your permission, I'd like to say just a few words about that.

"What we at the DI are searching for is a politics of authenticity. By that I mean a way to translate the insights expressed by Alice just a moment ago into an actual political program, and an actual way of living. How to go about achieving that—at this point, I don't know any more than you do. But I can cite you some interesting stats for the period of the last four months. Consumer sales are down more than 30 percent. A movement has arisen in the military, of courageous individuals refusing to serve in what they correctly call 'America's imperialist wars.' [Applause] The sale of antidepressant drugs has fallen off by nearly 40 percent. And finally, as of last Thursday, membership in the DI topped the 1 million mark. [Huge applause] So something is happening in this country, although it's too soon to tell where it will lead.

"Politicans of the two major political parties often say that what is at stake in the next election, and the next, and the next, is the soul of America. The reason it's always at stake is that the two parties are virtually identical. They offer no real change in our way of life, and so the soul of America remains rotten. It's a cruel soul, one that makes it illegal to feed the homeless, that approves of torture, that loves the death penalty, and that defines life as a competition, as winning out over the other guy. It's a soul that doesn't know its next-door neighbor, that leaves its children to fend for themselves, and that hasn't the simple ability to see another person's point of view. It's a soul that elects sociopaths to office—people like Nixon, Reagan, the Bushes, Bill Clinton, and Obama. What we are asking is that all this stop; that we apologize to every country we have destroyed, from Guatemala to Vietnam to Iraq; that we close down Madison Avenue and the peddling of false desires; that we put an end to the corporate rape of nature and the insane program of endless economic expansion; the list goes on and on.

"In order to do this, we need changes at the individual level, of the kind reflected in the statistics I just read off. But we also, I think, need a political party with real muscle, one that numbers in the millions. The DI has 1 million members today; perhaps it will have 2 million next month. One can only hope. What can I say, beyond: tell your friends. And tomorrow, be kind to just one person. Good night, and thank you for coming."

The standing ovation lasted about twenty minutes. The five of us lined up on stage, held hands, and took a bow. Dozens of people released balloons, which floated up to the ceiling and formed a canopy. A golden moment, if there ever was one.

16.

Trevor's timing for buying me a bulletproof vest and making me wear it couldn't have been better. Two days after the MSG event there was an attempt on my life, at a lecture I was giving in Chicago. The initial impact of the bullet on my chest knocked me down, after which the shooter—one Orlando Lima, a Colombian national living in the US, who had a record as a small-time drug dealer—was overwhelmed by security and taken into custody. He wouldn't say much; he was obviously a hired gun. But who, we all wondered, had hired him?

The Chicago PD, of course, is not particularly known for a gentle approach to interrogations, and Sr. Lima finally confessed to having been paid $1 million to snuff me out: half in advance, half upon delivery. He never saw the second half, obviously, and I wondered how bright the guy was, thinking he could kill someone in public and not get nailed. But the police had a hard time believing his story, which was that he was contacted by two executives, one from Noxia and the other from Floogle, to do the job. Could these two digital giants have been so clumsy? And would they really have regarded me as a threat, to the point of hiring a hit man? It seemed fantastic. Lima, in any case, stuck to his story, but said he wouldn't name names (and would they have been real names, in any case?), nor would he agree to testify in court, unless he was granted full immunity and put in the witness protection program. "Unless you disappear me," he told the detectives, "I'm dead meat."

Of course, corporate executives can do virtually anything they want, in terms of white collar crime, and walk away unscathed; but this was crime of a different order. The FBI got in on the case, and under threat of having their entire American operations closed down, the companies caved. They surrendered the two executives, insisting that no one higher up on the food chain knew of the plot (dubious), and the men eventually wound up serving lengthy prison terms. This time, the major newspapers couldn't look the other way.

Which is how, *mirabile dictu,* I wound up on the front cover of *Time Magazine,* under the banner "The Man Who Said No." The magazine did a long essay on the DI, even going so far as to reprint the entire Mission Statement. Philip Roth was quoted as saying, "I'm certainly glad the would-be assassins were brought to justice, but the event validates everything Professor Haskel has been arguing about existential strain. This is capitalism gone off its rocker, in my opinion." Bill Maher also weighed in, adding that "George Haskel has an open invitation to come back on my show any time he wants."

Back home, the five of us sat around in utter amazement. Martin was the first to speak.

"What is it, Trev: you've got a crystal ball? You told George to get a bulletproof vest; said Noxia and Floogle would come after him; and predicted he'd make the front cover of *Time Magazine.* Have you got some sort of pipeline to God, or what?"

"More like to the devil," said Alice. "What have we entered, the Twilight Zone? George?"

"I'm too tired to speak," I replied.

"First your head, now your chest," said Trevor. "And with each hit, we're doing better and better. Although it's rather a high price to pay, I grant you. Needless to say, George, we're all relieved you're still alive. But clearly, we need greater protection than a vest. The DI has tapped into something really dark and primal in America, and this attack is not likely to be the last of it."

"That's one enormous I-told-you-so," said Alice. "So what do we do next?"

"Hire a bodyguard," ventured Paola. "Maybe two of them. We also need to buy a bulletproof car."

"Spoken like a true Sicilian," said Martin, but then added quickly, "No, you're right, of course. What's a car like that gonna cost us?"

"I have a hunch," said Alice, "that we just might be able to afford it."

She was right. Within another month, the DI membership shot up to 2 million. We bought the car, hired the bodyguards, and I felt like I was living in a gilded cage.

Overnight, I became a major public figure. Reporters from European and Japanese newspapers came to Takoma Park to interview me; I was on dozens of TV shows, in the US and (via cable) overseas. The DI officially registered the Authentic Party, and we announced that I would be running in the next presidential election, three years hence. I was endorsed by Roth/Franzen/Turkle/Maher, of course, but also by Pope Francis, the National Council of Churches, and the American Psychiatric Association.

"You've talked about Dada and Surrealism," said Martin; "well, now you're living it."

My own problem was that I both did and did not want what was happening. Quite by accident, I had awoken a sleeping giant, and now the opportunity to fundamentally alter American culture lay before me, before us, as a real possibility. On the other hand, my life as a private citizen was over. And did I really want to be president? I couldn't imagine I'd make a good one. I'd be 74 when I took office, and frankly, I was tired. This was not what I had imagined for my retirement.

"Hey," said Alice that evening, when I told her all this, "no one told you to make mincemeat out of Hillary and Colton Farnsworth. That was your decision. You let the genie out of the bottle, my love. Now all of us have to deal with it. As for me, just so you know, I have no regrets. Meanwhile, I'll need to check out the cost of renting Yankee Stadium. Holds 48,000, don't you know. Of course, there's always the National Mall."

"I have a dream?"

"Well you do, George, you do."

The Fabulous Five reconvened the next day.

"George," said Paola, "my father actually knows the Italian ambassador to the UN. Do you want me to try to get you an invitation to address it?"

"Oh for fuck's sake," I blurted out. "Next I'll be an astronaut. Sorry, Paola, I didn't mean to snap at you. I'd just like to try to keep it simple, if it's at all possible at this point. Where are we on Trevor's checklist?"

Trev pulled it out. "Let's see...Well, we certainly accomplished item number five, getting George on the front cover of *Time*. Sorry! [He made a face.] Also three and four: speaking to high schools, and mounting a major event, namely the forum at NYU. That leaves Paola's mural, and George's book of the same name. Paola, how's the oil business coming along?"

"Just about done, My Fountain." She turned to us. "I call him Fountain because his name reminds me of the Fontana di Trevi in Rome, where all wishes come true."

"Jesus, you guys," said Martin; "get a room."

"We already have one, carino. Anyway, I can finish it up this week. Do you want me to roll it up and ship it down in a tube, or would you prefer to come up to New York?"

"Let's go to New York," I said, "all four of us. We could use a break. We could stay at a nice hotel, have a bowl of borscht at the Russian Tea Room, walk around Central Park, and go to the MOMA. What do you think?"

"And the bodyguards?" Alice inquired.

"I'm afraid they come with us," I replied.

"I'd better get home and start painting," said Paola. "See you guys next weekend."

"Wait," said Trevor; "I'm coming with you."

Martin smiled, and sang: "That's *amore*!"

17.

Happily, Trevor forgot to ask me how I was coming along with the book, inasmuch as I had zero pages written. But I needed to rest my brain, and just veg out in New York. I promised myself I'd start in on the thing when we got back to Maryland. Jesus, here I was, seventy-one years old, had been beaten and shot at and was working like a dog. I kept wondering when the family heart attack pattern would finally do me in. "Take me now, O Lord!" Did I really mean it? No.

Meanwhile, Alice suggested I spend the week before New York doing a podcast. "It'll be good practice for the book," she insisted, "and also, given your fame, any major radio station will pick it up. It will also be a chance for you to update the Mission Statement, and say more about what we believe in, what we hope to accomplish."

Reluctantly, I agreed. It actually got broadcast over a large number of radio stations, as well as getting posted on the Net. As follows:

Truth in Advertising

By George Haskel

Hello, everybody; this is George Haskel. As many of you know, the Dullness Institute recently launched a legitimate political party, called the Authentic Party, and I shall be running for president in the next presidential election. I realize it's a bit early to start campaigning, but I wanted to share my thoughts with you as to what the AP is all about, and what I envision for America. I would also love to have your reactions, which can be sent to Alice Connors at the DI web site.

Some wag once wrote that an institution was a place to not get done what you say you are trying to do. This is my great fear now for the DI and the AP. Once things become large, and become official, there is a tendency to also become ossified; to lose one's original purpose, or even betray it. Should this happen to us—and it could—that would be a great tragedy, in my opinion. My original vision was born out of revulsion, a disgust at what America had become, and at the way we were living. I saw Americans as being miserable because they had bought into a definition of success called the American Dream, which consisted of hustling, competing, getting ahead, and pursuing wealth or fame. And I knew that real success was a very different thing: it consisted in the relationship you had with yourself. As John Ruskin once put it, "There is no wealth but life." If you let yourself be defined from the outside, it will eventually make you sick. Unfortunately, this is what most Americans have chosen to do.

So I began to talk about authenticity because I was sure that this was the key to turning one's life around. And on the individual level, that may be fine. But friends and colleagues and many of you wrote in, and asked me if this vision couldn't be implemented on a *political* level; sociology as well as psychology, if you will. And so I began to think about it. I didn't have to think very long, as it turned out. The police riot in Alexandria, the assassination attempt in Chicago—well, events overtook us, at the DI, and we are now plunged into political issues whether we want to be or not.

Exactly what I shall do if I become your president, I cannot say at this time, beyond telling you that I would do my best to dismantle the structures of power and greed: corporate, governmental, and military. A tall order, for sure. And it does come down to a fight for the soul of America—for your souls. The Republicrat Party cannot give you back your soul, inasmuch as they lost theirs long ago. I think everyone knows that by now. Its only interest is in money and power and war and manipulation, and that you remain docile and keep them in office. What I hope the AP will be able to offer you is a rich life—by which I mean rich in spirit, not in cash. I cannot, and do not wish to, impose this on you; I can only succeed if you want what I'm offering. But the details of that are for another day.

What I'd like to offer today are some caveats regarding potential stumbling blocks along the way. Here they are.

1. We have talked a lot about love, about treating others right, and about not giving in to existential strain. This is all well and good, but let's be realistic: you can't love everyone; this is just not possible. It doesn't mean you have to hate them, of course, but pressuring people into love doesn't have much chance of success.

Some of you know that I'm a big fan of *Seinfeld*. There was one episode called "The Bizarro Jerry," in which Elaine discovers a mirror image of Jerry's world. Jerry's world, of course, is very funny, but if you look more closely, you see that everyone is hustling and competing. Rather than support each other, they are constantly mocking each other, scoring points off one another. The trio Elaine discovers is one in which the three individuals are kind to each other and to other people. They are clean and organized; they read books; they give money to the homeless; they buy each other groceries, or fight to pick up the check in restaurants. They are, in a word, authentic, whereas Jerry & Co. are dishonest and manipulative. So Elaine deserts Jerry's world for the Bizarro world, but she soon discovers a significant drawback: the guys are *too* good. They are lovey-dovey to the point that you want to barf. It's just too cloying, too goody two-shoes. They reject her, in any case, and she returns to her normal inauthentic life; which, sadly enough, is authentic to her.

My point is that we at the DI are interested in reality, not in manipulating ourselves into being sweet. We aren't Esalen or Scientology or Oprah; we aren't politically correct; and we regard the New Age as a bad joke. So be clear about that if you wish to join us: authenticity means honesty, and that's what we embrace.

2. Authenticity requires the right context if it is to have any meaning. For a short while, I was doing authenticity seminars for large corporations, only to discover that for them it was just a tool. Their goal was money and power, and they were interested in authenticity only to the extent that it enabled them to hustle more efficiently. They had no interest in authenticity for its own sake.

The same thing is true of the political left, the "progressive" crowd, for whom "revolution" and left-wing political activity is frequently a means of enlarging their egos: "I make the revolution and therefore I AM," as Doris Lessing once put it. In my dealings with many of these folks, I found that they were as selfish and manipulative and narcissistic as the corporate executives I worked with. They are, however, quite correct in their critique of the the structures of power, about which I'll say more in a minute.

My point here is: don't be fooled. Pick the right context in which to be authentic. Otherwise, it's just more of what we already have. Anyone can mimic the language of authenticity, after all.

3. My third caveat concerns the problem of getting hung up on form rather than content.' We at the DI have never sold T-shirts and coffee mugs, and we won't be doing it for the AP either. Slavoj Žižek famously said to the Occupy movement: «Don't fall in love with yourselves!"; which is precisely what they proceeded to do. It's very human, of course, to want to show off: see, my AP bumper sticker proclaims that I am a good person. This is a kind of secular fundamentalism in which, as with the Pharisees of old, you get obsessed with the symbolism and pay very little attention to *behaving* authentically. Of course, no one is perfect, and we need to cut each other some slack. But if you are seeking to buy AP underwear or pasta sauce, then this is the wrong political party for you. Authenticity is not a fetish. In a word, as Žižek was telling Occupy, don't go overboard. Any ideology, taken too far, tends to turn into its opposite, turn against itself; Christianity and Communism are classic instances of this. Seek balance in your authenticity, rather than devotion.

4. The last caveat is what I referred to a moment ago: the "progressive" analysis of the structures of power. These structures are real, and they are killing all of us, the planet included. Authenticity may require confronting them and struggling against them, and perhaps developing alternative institutional structures to replace those of capitalism, as the latter continues to fail. But I personally am hoping to undermine them in a different way. Big Pharma, Noxia, Floogle, General Motors, the military, Wall Street—all of these continue to exist only because we buy into the American Dream, the world of hustling and consumerism. Reject that Dream, and all of these institutions would be seriously threatened. It's a question of microcosm and macrocosm: if individual behavior changes en masse, these structures of power may start to crumble. Or at least, that's my hope. All we can do is try to have a better life, which is to say, a real one.

Thank you, and godspeed.

18.

And so, New York. We decided to drive up in the bulletproof car, bodyguards and all. What the heck. I must admit I have a soft spot for New York; hustling aside, it always felt to me like the most European of American cities.

"Where are we staying?" asked Martin (we picked him up in Baltimore, on the way up).

"The Edison Hotel," I told him. "It's in Times Square. Comfortable, but not luxurious. Also very Jewish; you'll like it."

"How is a hotel 'very Jewish'? They offer free circumcisions, or what?" Alice burst out laughing.

"More like matzo ball soup in the restaurant on the ground floor. Decent pastrami as well."

"Will we be flinging sandwiches at the NYPD, then?"

"Not this time," I said. "Though I always felt bad that they jumped us in Alexandria. No time to unwrap and throw, when you're getting unexpectedly clobbered."

"Have you ever considered the possibility that you're insane?"

Martin asked me.

"I did, but I rejected it. By the way, I asked Paola to fix you up with a girlfriend of hers, a therapist, stunning blonde, according to Paola. About forty years old."

"WHAT?"

Alice: "Martin, don't be alarmed. We thought you might be unhappy, being a fifth wheel. Much better we should all triple date. Plus, you'll be among friends, so no pressure. I bet you'll like her."

"What's her name?"

"Phoebe Buffet. No, just kidding. Carrie Flanagan. Irish descent. Drinks a lot. No, just kidding."

"I'm going to strangle you, Alice," said Martin. "Do you know what her brand of therapy is?"

"Yes, she's a sex therapist. No, just kidding. I don't know; you'll have to ask her."

"George, would you please control your woman?"

I laughed. "I wish."

Including the detour in Baltimore, it tooks us about six hours to get to the Edison Hotel and park the car. The bodyguards were in one room, Martin in another, and Alice and I in a third. I was still having a hard time getting used to having the two guards following me around, and had suggested that we dispense with them, that the danger had passed; but Trevor wouldn't hear of it. He was convinced there was going to be another attempt on my life, sooner or later. Who am I to argue with a psychic with a proven track record?, I thought.

"Dinner at eight in Brooklyn," Alice announced. "An Italian

restaurant, naturally. I Tre Porcellini, or something like that."

"So I'll huff and I'll puff?" I asked her. She ignored me.

"Anyway, time for a nap and a shower," said Alice. "We depart at six. I want some time to look at Paola's work and, of course, the mural."

We got to Paola's studio a little before seven. Carrie, the Irish therapist, was going to meet us at the restaurant. Trevor was there, of course; meanwhile, Paola had covered up the canvas with a large sheet, so as to execute a proper unveiling. We lined up on a bench in front of it.

"OK, you guys, here goes. I give you 'Truth in Advertising'!"

Trevor had already seen it; the rest of us sat there transfixed. It was something of a departure for Paola, because it wasn't entirely nonrepresentational. It started out with dark swirls of color at the lower left, and swept across the diagonal to the upper right. The line of the diagonal was a brilliant green stem, that issued out in a large yellow rose. On the lower right was something that looked like a crown of thorns, with a few drops of blood beneath it. I was speechless.

"Is this a good silence or a bad silence?" Paola finally asked us.

"*Jenseits von Gut und Böse*," I replied.

"Che?"

"Nietzsche: Beyond good and evil. It's wonderful, it's terrible, it's magnificent. I don't know how you did it."

"It's amazing, Paola," said Martin. "Somehow, I don't know exactly how, it's about authenticity."

"We've got to get this displayed asap," said Alice. "Either at a major gallery, or else on a large wall, outside. I'll start checking out the possibilities when we get back home."

We made our way to I Tre Porcellini. Carrie Flanagan was already there, and Paola introduced her to the group. She was very cute, pert, slim, sexy. Green eyes, delicate hands. I sneaked a peak at Martin, but couldn't gauge his reaction. I couldn't imagine he was disappointed.

We ordered champagne, and toasted Paola and "Truth in Advertising." After a while Martin and Carrie got into a private conversation—always a good sign—and the four of us left them alone, to get acquainted. "This is going to work," Paola whispered; "Carrie is three months out of a relationship, and just about ready to meet a nice guy. I'm told the Irish-Jewish mix is quite a compatible one."

And so the champagne flowed, and then the vino rosso. I got quite drunk, which amused Alice no end. Platters of spezzatino and salad and pizza and tiramisu floated by in an unending procession. "A toast!" I cried. "To authenticity in Italian cooking!"

"George," said Alice, "you're shit-faced." "To being authentically shit-faced!" I cried. And so the evening went. Alice and I finally drove back to the Edison, leaving Martin and Carrie to continue their engrossing conversation (read: mating dance).

"He'll probably get laid," I mumbled to no one in particular.

"You're such a romantic, George. It's why I love you."

"Just trying to be authentic," I said. "Truth in Advertising."

19.

I stayed home over the next few weeks, trying to expand the podcast into an entire book. Alice worked on finding a gallery or location for the mural; Trevor and Martin devoted themselves to DI finances, AP organizing, and arrangements for lectures and interviews. (The demand rate was now up to something like thirty per week.) Paola came down on weekends, and helped with all of it. And Martin and Carrie, the hopeless lovebirds, traded weekends in New York and Baltimore, with side visits to Takoma Park.

What can I say, dear reader? We were as happy as pigs in shit.

One problem we were having, however, was at the individual level, namely helping members detox from their inauthentic lives. Switching to authenticity after years of b.s. can feel like stepping off a cliff, and many people phoned us in various states of panic. We had to expand our phone lines, and hire a number of therapists to take the occasional desperate calls. Via a long-distance hookup, Carrie Flanagan was now on staff as well. Trevor was especially good at handling these situations; everybody's best friend, I liked to call him. Meanwhile, the membership was also working out their anxieties in our seminars, which were running on a daily basis, seven days a week.

And then another major breakthrough occurred: Senator Alex Robbins from New York, who lived, of course, in DC, showed up, asking for private therapy sessions. It had to be hush-hush, for the time being; he was a Democrat, and he was giving serious thought to running for reelection, in three years, on the Authentic Party ticket. Clearly, this would be a coup of major proportions. I decided to handle his case myself.

"Why are you here?" is how I usually began working with someone. In this case, it was pretty straightforward: Robbins wondered whether, if he chose to live an authentic life, he would be able to remain in politics, or would instead have to move to some organic farm in Upstate New York and start growing vegetables. I laughed.

"No way of knowing ahead of time," I told him. "But you don't have to do everything all at once, right? Paso a paso. I should add that neither the DI nor the AP is into telling people what they should do. That's for *you* to decide. Our job is only to open the possibility of an authentic life, so you have a clear picture of what that would entail. Then you will be able to make an informed decision as to how you want to proceed. Does that make sense?"

This calmed him down somewhat, and we agreed on a schedule of two sessions per week. I decided to share his conundrum with the group at our next meeting, to get their input.

"Look," I said, "this may be a rare opportunity for us. Senator Robbins is an unusual guy. He's asking us to help him become an authentic politician, but he's worried that it's an oxymoron, like 'business ethics.' And I don't know the answer; I just told him we'd find out along the way. But if he succeeds, maybe the infection could spread. Maybe we could work with other senators or congressmen. Or am I crazy?"

"But you gave him an authentic answer," said Trevor, "namely that he would find out along the way. Anything else would have been dishonest."

"OK, then," I said, "I'll keep you guys posted."

It didn't take long for Robbins to hit a wall. It came in the form of a vote pending in the Senate on expanding military operations and facilities in New York State. A yes vote—assuming the bill passed—meant tons of money and jobs for New York, and thus the strong likelihood of his being reelected three years hence. A no vote on his part, regardless of the outcome, probably meant his career was over.

"You see, George, the line we politicos always take is that even if we cast a vote we believe is wrong—morally wrong, which is how I see it in this case—if it means we stay in office, then it's worth the price, because then we can do good things in other areas. The problem is that those other areas usually involve questionable moral decisions as well, leading to yet another compromise; until finally, you never really get to do any good, and the purpose is nothing more than power, i.e. staying in office for its own sake. There's nothing more inauthentic than that, right?"

"Alex," I told him, "as I see it, if you vote for military appropriations, you don't really have to say anything on the Senate floor; you just vote. But if you vote against them, you might want to prepare a speech; which is something you and I can work on together, if you would like. How authentic you wish to be in that speech would be up to you, but the decision of a yes vote versus a no vote has to come first."

"George, the US defense budget is the largest in the world. It amounts to something like the combined defense budgets of the next ten nations below us. Furthermore, it's hardly a *defense* budget; the US military is just an imperial army, destroying defenseless countries so as to further its own economic and geopolitical aims. These so-called Islamic threats we're always talking about: we created them! We fucked with the Middle East for decades, until they finally got fed up and struck back. Then we get all indignant about it, as if we wouldn't have done the same thing if the tables were turned—which is what we did with the British in 1776." Sweat was pouring off his face.

"Well, Alex, that's the authentic speech, if you want to give it. Beyond a doubt, it will end your political career. Let me ask you this: If that happens, what will you do?"

"Go back to practicing law, I suspect," he answered.

"Did you ever think of coming to work for us? Not that we can pay you a whole lot, but at least the work would line up with your own values. Meanwhile, you would have three years to wreak a lot of havoc among your colleagues, perhaps even convert a few of them. And then you could run for Senate again, but on the AP ticket; though you'd probably lose, as will I." I smiled. "Anyway, that's what authenticity looks like in this case. The decision is up to you."

Alex laughed. "Man, you really do create problems for people, don't you?"

"Well, we try," I said, smiling again. "I've never hid the fact that authenticity comes with a price, and sometimes it's high. What does your wife want you to do, by the way?"

"Oh, she's in your camp all the way, ever since the day that Bill Maher hugged you. If I vote no, we'd probably have a second honeymoon." He laughed. "I guess there's an upside to authenticity as well."

"More than you know, Alex; more than you know."

Alex voted no, made his "Enough imperialism!" speech on the Senate floor, and was subsequently ostracized by most of Washington. Most, but not all. There were actually a few senators who were silently in his camp, whom he intended to work on; and meanwhile, both he and his wife, June, began working for the DI/AP on a volunteer basis. We had scored a major victory; the infection was now starting to spread among political circles.

20.

Just about this time, we got a break on the mural. The curator at the Swank Feinstein Gallery on West 57th Street visited Paola in her studio, saw the mural along with her other work, and offered her a one-woman show.

"All of it is brilliant," she told Paola. "Over a three-week period, I'm sure we would be able to sell most of it. Even less our commission, you would do quite well. The large piece, I understand, will be on display but not for sale; but its power will go far to establish you as one of America's leading artists."

Paola was ecstatic. But as the days went by, she began to have her doubts. She phoned Alice about it.

"Alice, honey, I can't help thinking that Swank Feinstein is a little too rich for my blood. Oh, the curator went on about how the exhibition would put me on the map and line my pockets and so on, but I'm feeling that doing a painting on authenticity and then hanging it in a gallery for the rich would be terribly inauthentic. However, it's the only offer we've gotten, and it would at least put the mural on display."

"It's your painting, Paola, so it's your decision," said Alice.

"No, it's *our* painting, it's the Institute's painting. It has to be a group decision, as far as I'm concerned."

"Paola, can I make a suggestion, just something for you to think about, before we discuss it this weekend? One of the most authentic parts of the US, in my opinion, and one that just happens to be soaking in murals, is the Mission District in San Francisco. It's gritty, real people leading real lives. I suggest you and I fly out to San Francisco with slides of the painting and show it to the City Council. Or we could just send them photos of it online. If they approve, we could arrange to mount it in a very public place, outdoors."

"It's a great idea, Alice, but won't we be running the danger of it being defaced, or torn down?"

"Defaced, probably not. The murals painted on the walls of the Mission have acquired a rather sacred aura; they don't tend to get vandalized. But if we pasted your painting onto a wall, you're right, some people might want to tear it down; I don't know. We need to think about it some more."

We convened for a discussion on Saturday morning. Paola explained the situation with Swank Feinstein, the possibility of locating it in the Mission instead, and her concern about having it torn off the wall.

"Here's a thought," said Trevor; "why not both?"

"Both what?" Paola asked.

"Both locations, the Mission and Swank Feinstein."

"Because there's only one painting," said Paola.

"Only one painting *now*," said Trevor. "I'm just going to put in my two cents here, and let you and the others decide. Here's how I see it. First, there is nothing wrong with an artist making a living. Earning a living isn't hustling; it's just being a mature adult professional who gets fair wage for her work.

Hustling is something else: it's being on the make, having no limits, and that's not what's going on here. Authenticity doesn't necessarily mean poverty. So, I would say, tell Swank Feinstein yes, but for now sell only your other work, not the mural; which is what you and the curator already agreed on. The mural may come in handy later, like during George's political campaign.

"Second, show the SF City Council slides of the thing, or send them photos online, and explain that you would like to reproduce it on a wall in the Mission. It won't be identical to the original, obviously, but it probably will be close enough."

"I agree completely," I put in. "There's no reason not to do two paintings and put them in two locations. Of course, Paola, doing another mural is a lot of work, and we'll all understand if you don't—"

"I'll do it," she said; "of course I'll do it. Trev's idea is spot-on."

"OK, then," I said; "next step is for us to contact the SF City Council, and if necessary go out there with slides. You and Alice, I mean. Sound good? Meanwhile, my own vote on Swank Feinstein is yes." With which, everyone agreed.

"Anything else?" I asked.

"Yes," said Paola; "Trev and I are getting married." She took a lovely engagement ring out of her pocket and put it on her finger. An uproar ensued.

"How? When did you decide? Where?"—we fell over each other with questions.

"Oh," said Paola, "Trev and I have discussed it for a while now, and in the midst of those discussions I got pregnant. In seven months I'm going to give birth to the world's first authentic baby. It's going to be a boy, and his name will be Mario—Mario Jones." She was beaming; Trevor sort of blushed.

"You dog, you," Martin said to him.

"Fantastico, ragazza!" I exclaimed. "I'm going out right now to buy champagne for us to have with dinner tonight. There's nothing like toting champagne in a bulletproof car, eh wot?"

"Works for me," said Alice. "You get the bubbly, and I'll e-mail San Fran."

21.

As it turned out, Alice and Paola didn't have to go to San Francisco to pitch the mural to the City Council. Serendipitously, Jerry Brown, the governor of California, wrote me two days later inviting me to address the California state legislature. I immediately wrote back accepting the invitation, and asking him about the possibility of the DI painting a mural on a wall in the Mission District. He asked to see the pics online, which were duly sent, and he phoned me the next day.

"Done deal, George; the work is fabulous. My office will pay Paola's airfare and put her up for two weeks at a B&B in the Mission. Sound OK?"

"More than OK, governor. By the way, have you ever thought of switching to the Authentic Party? I mean, you of all people, governor; you've been pursuing authenticity all your life."

"You flatter me, George, but I would be being inauthentic if I said I didn't like it. I have to be in DC about two weeks from now. How about you have me over for dinner?"

"Another done deal, governor. You give me the date and tell me what you'd like to eat, and we'll take it from there."

We hung up the phone. "That Jerry," I said out loud; "what a guy."

Paola flew out to San Francisco a few days later, and spent nearly two weeks on a scaffold, painting "Truth in Advertising II." She had a large photo of Version I with her, to jog her memory, and the result was pretty close to the original, except with a slightly Hispanic twist. It was a huge hit in the neighborhood, with little kids running back and forth underneath the scaffold, calling out to Paola in Spanish. Authenticity at its finest. The day after it was done, I flew to SF and stood in front of a lectern on a windy day.

"¡Hola, y gracias por venir!" I began. "Estoy muy contento estar aquí." The crowd whistled and cheered. I switched to English.

"My friends, we are here to honor a great painting, and also a great artist, Paola Marini. As most of you know, Paola and I are members of the Authentic Party, and I will be running in the presidential election three years from now. So I want to take this occasion to officially launch the AP in California. I also want to add that two days ago, your governor, Jerry Brown, had dinner at my home in Takoma Park, Maryland, and he gave me permission to say that he agrees with the philosophy of the AP, and that he will be endorsing my run for the presidency." [Huge applause] Is it possible to be an authentic politician? I think it is. Jerry is one, as is Senator Alex Robbins of New York. And our numbers will grow, you can count on it, and I hope you will join us. [More applause]

"Speaking of authenticity, some of you may have seen that Kevin Costner film called *McFarland, USA*, which is the true story of a track coach named Jim White who takes a job at a high school in McFarland, in the Central Valley. He had a great impact on his Hispanic students, taking them to victory in the cross-country state championship in 1987, and encouraging them to go to college so that they wouldn't have to remain *recolectores*—fruit and vegetable pickers—for the rest of their lives. But the film derives its real power from the impact that the students and their families have on *him*. All he ever thought of up to that point was material success, moving up the economic ladder. He had absolutely no interest in any other form of success, which might include friendship, loyalty, and community; these were completely alien notions to him. But the town embraces him and his family. A neighbor gives him a chicken. The Díaz family has him over for dinner and stuffs him with enchiladas. The town makes a *quinceañera* for his older daughter. And finally, when a rich white high school in Palo Alto offers him the 'perfect' job, he turns it down, and he lives in McFarland to this day.

"What happened? White was given the choice between hustling and authenticity, and although it was difficult, he chose the latter. Love had entered his heart; the Mexican community had managed to turn him into a human being.

"It is this that the AP stands for. Let me be clear: we are not opposed to economic success; not at all. There is dignity in well-paid work. The problem arises when that's *all* one is interested in, and when the pursuit of money and power—such as we see in Washington today—takes over one's entire life. What then happens is that authentic life, including caring for other people, gets pushed aside, and the result is an emptiness at the center. This is what has happened to America, and it has cost us dearly. We really don't know who we are any more. The barrio of the Mission, it seems to me, thus has a lot to teach the rest of the country. I hope I shall have your support in restoring authenticity to American life.

"Gracias."

Needless to say, it was a good day.

22.

The exhibition of the mural at the Swank Feinstein Gallery was a rather different affair, as the reader might imagine. A subdued evening, with martinis and canapés; très chic. I showed up in a three-piece suit, and made no speeches. Alex Robbins was also there for the opening, with his wife. During the three weeks that the paintings were shown, Paola's belly increased gently in size, and her wallet increased dramatically. The mural got featured in an article in the *New Yorker*, along with some mildly favorable discussion of the AP. It was good: more exposure, new members, greater visibility. We were now a "presence" on both the East and West Coasts.

Well, perhaps more than just a presence. Unbeknownst to me, Paola did have her father contact the Italian ambassador to the UN, who then contacted the Secretary-General. The result was that I was invited to address the General Assembly. I chose as the title of my talk, "The Choice Before Us Today." As soon as the date was set for the talk, the Fab Five convened in Takoma Park to discuss it.

"George," said Martin, "this is really the big leagues. You're not standing on a chair with a megaphone on the Alexandria waterfront anymore. You're on the front cover of *Time*. The governor of California comes to your house for dinner. You have a senator in your camp. And now, you will be addressing the representatives of something like 200 nations. What do you want to say to them, and what sort of opportunity is this for us, do you think?"

"Martin, I tell you honestly, I still feel like I'm a no-account retired professor of German literature, a loner not sure of what to do with the rest of his life. How did I wind up with a gorgeous and talented girlfriend [blush from Alice], and friends like you guys, in my life? Everything seems like it happened by accident, and it *did* happen by accident: Bill Maher, the Alexandria police, near-death in Chicago—we've got quite a list here. I don't really feel like I did any of it. I feel like I channeled it, or that it just passed through me.

"And actually, I think that's good. I regard ego as highly inauthentic, a serious loss of perspective. None of us is all that important, after all. That's why I keep saying that the DI or AP has to be about the ideas, not about me. Because maybe humility—true humility, not false modesty—is the key to it all. I mean, who am I, really, to be addressing the UN? All I have is a certain feeling for life, and perhaps some talent in being able to articulate it. So what's next? The Nobel Prize?"

"Don't rule it out," Trevor interjected.

"How many people in this world," said Martin, "do you think, have those two things, i.e. a certain feeling for life, and the ability to articulate it? A few hundred? Do you seriously think you have nothing to offer the members of the General Assembly?"

"It'll probably come off as platitudes, which no one—rightly—should pay any attention to."

"George," said Paola, "you chose as the title of your talk, 'The Choice Before Us Today.' What did you mean by that?"

"I guess that human beings on the planet today are caught between living their own lives vs. living someone else's version of what their lives should be," I responded. "And let's face it, most people don't have a choice. They are *forced* to live out someone else's version, because they are trapped in sweat shops, or slavery, which still exists, or the sex trade, or the consumerist fog that blankets Europe and America, or some totalitarian regime. And what really sucks is that when there is an uprising against this injustice, à la Colton Farnsworth, the revolution just turns out to be a revolving door, a new set of masters, a new set of buzzwords, and the same relations of power and abuse that obtained before."

"You're right," said Paola, "but that vision is much too dark. After all, what we're trying to do at the DI is alter sensibilities person by person and group by group. Look at the constellation of characters we've managed to draw into our energy field. The list now includes major politicians. And I tell you honestly, George, I don't agree with you that it's all been accidental. It's been *you*, George. You have a way of reaching people that is uncanny, that changes them. That's why all of us are sitting here today. And you pass that ability on to others. So why not go to the UN, explain the model of social change we're working on at the DI, and suggest that they experiment with it in their own countries?"

"Jesus, Paola," said Alice, "I'm thinking maybe *you* should give that talk at the UN."

"Fine by me," I put in. "Seriously, Paola, that's terrific, and I agree with you 95 percent. My 5 percent of hesitation is that Americans have an annoying habit of telling the rest of the world what to do, and I don't want to come off as one more pushy gringo."

The discussion went on all day long, during which time I took the opportunity to phone Jerry Brown and Alex Robbins to get their take on the matter. In the end, we all agreed that the crucial point about giving other nations an American formula lay not in what I said but in how I said it. All I could say, really, was something like "This is what the AP is trying to implement in the United States; if you think it might be valuable or appropriate to your own situation, feel free to adopt it."

"After all," added Alice, "we've made a big point of saying that we can't impose authenticity on anyone; we can only offer it as an option."

Which is what I finally wound up doing. I spoke for about forty-five minutes, and tried to be as low-key as possible; though I found myself becoming a bit strident at the end. "That famous line from Rilke," I said, "applies to our own situation: 'You must change your life.' Half the world's population lives on less than two dollars a day. So it comes down to this: to act, or not to act. It's up to you. If you choose the latter, it won't be very long before we don't have a world to live in."

I felt it was a platitude; I felt they had heard it all before, and I believed the likely outcome for most of my audience would be that they would choose not to act. What the hell, you do what you can. I decided it was time for me to return to domestic politics; the entire world was more than I could handle.

23.

Reactions to the talk were mixed, as was to be expected. A number of newspapers called it "lame," but there were a few that regarded it as courageous. *Le Monde* wrote: "Sure, we've heard it all before, but given the state of the world, we need to hear it again, until people do take M. Haskel's advice and act—which is what he is doing in his own country. We applaud him."

At our Saturday morning meeting, Paola declared, "You see? Even the hypercritical French say you were great. You put the challenge precisely, and that's exactly what was needed."

"Well," I said, "I guess we can never know what effect our words can have, down the line. But now that that's behind us, what's next on the list? Trev?"

"Let's not dismiss the UN too quickly," he countered. "I mean, you *are* a major figure now, and you *did* give a speech at the United Nations. We need to parlay that into something larger, or equally large. Or else consolidate our gains."

"How do you mean?" asked Martin.

"Consider our list of allies, "said Trevor. "Jerry Brown, Alex

Robbins, Bill Maher, Sherry Turkle, Philip Roth, Jonathan Franzen. This is pretty impressive," he went on. "Why don't we approach these folks and ask them if they'd be willing to be on an Advisory Council for Restructuring America. Then we need to add, say, four to six more famous people. Why not Woody Allen, for example? Or Susan Sarandon?"

"OK, so let's say we have a Council of ten famous people. Then what?" said Martin.

"Then," responded Trevor, "we do a repeat of the NYU forum, but in every city in the US with a population in excess of 500,000 people. That's more than seventy cities. I don't think the thing now is to create another major event. It can get hokey, after a while. Our job now is to persuade people across the country that what we are offering could radically improve their lives. We need to return to the grass-roots level. We now have 2 million members; let's shoot for 4. And George, you need to get that book out already. Except, let's change the title. Not *Truth in Advertising*, which is a bit too arcane, but something like *A Primer of Authenticity*. People need a handbook, giving them concrete actions they can take to make their lives more authentic. Anyway, more seminars, more phone lines, more lectures for all of us, distribution of George's book, plus the Advisory Council moving from city to city. A blitz, in other words; a propaganda campaign."

"And then?" Martin inquired.

"That's when it gets interesting. We start to call out institutions for being inauthentic. We will need to hire some investigative reporters to ferret out the stories. We name names. We hire a few attorneys to defend us, in the event of lawsuits, and to mount our own lawsuits. In other words, once we have a huge popular base and an effective, ongoing propaganda machine, we go on the attack. We go toe-to-toe with our opponents, which consist of people in positions of power who are lying and stealing and abusing that power."

"But there are a number of web sites, like Common Dreams, that are doing that already," said Alice. "Why bother?"

"Three reasons," Trev replied. "First, they are pretty small potatoes. Who reads those web sites? Only a tiny percentage of the American public is in their ideological camp. Second, Common Dreams doesn't sue anyone, doesn't actually attack anyone. Third, they do what they do as part of an amorphous, left-wing campaign. But it's not *really* a campaign, is it, because it's not being done in the name of an actual political party. Once we have a large popular base, are identified with leading figures in film and politics and literature, and then go on the attack as a specific political party, we turn into a real threat. And by doing that, we start to become equal to the Dems or the GOP in terms of being a serious political alternative. This will shake things up like nothing else."

"You see why I'm marrying him?" said Paola.

"When is that, by the way?" asked Alice.

"Two weeks from now, Brooklyn City Hall. Be there or be square."

Everybody laughed. "Small ceremony, just you guys and Trev's and my immediate families. Then back to The Three Little Pigs for vino and vitello tonnato. Va bene?"

"Wouldn't miss it for the world, my dear," I told her. "Meanwhile, back at the ranch, I wholeheartedly approve of Trevor's master plan. However, assuming everyone else does, there will be a ton of work to do. We'll need to delegate responsibility and start working on each part of the project. I get the book done, Alice calls Woody Allen [chuckles all around], Martin hires more phone people and reporters and lawyers—"

"Hey, too much!" objected Martin.

"OK, Paola helps you with all that, and Trev sits around

weaving a huge web of mischief and intrigue. What say you all, mates?"

"Aye!" they cried.

"Paola, can I pat your belly?"

"Me too! Me too!"

And with that, the meeting was over.

24.

The next day, Sunday, I awoke from a dream that I guessed, in part, was inspired by yesterday's reference to Woody Allen. In the dream, I'm working with a group of people to overthrow the King, and we get caught. The punishment is to get our heads chopped off. When it's my turn, I say to the executioner, "Just a little off the top." He doesn't get the joke, so I have to explain it to him; after which, he cuts my head off. Later, the King comes to talk to me. I tell him: "I can't talk; I'm dead." He still wants to talk. There is a sense that he admires me, wants to learn something from me.

I had a good laugh. The line about "Just a little off the top" is from a vignette in Woody Allen's film, *Everything You Always Wanted to Know About Sex.* Woody plays the role of a court jester who has been fooling around with the Queen, and gets caught. He's dragged off to the chopping block, and as the executioner is about to lop off his head, he says this ridiculous line.

Six of us were present that morning, including Carrie Flanagan, who had come down from New York, so as we sat around having a leisurely breakfast, I said, "I'm glad Carrie is with us today; I had a strange dream last night that I'd like to tell you guys about, and hopefully Carrie and the rest of you can tell me what it means."

At this, everybody perked up. "Your dreams are my visions," said Martin.

"I don't know what that means," I replied.

"Neither do I," he said; "it just sounded good, I thought."

So I related the dream, and there was silence for a while. Finally Trevor said, "Well, there's an obvious reference to Woody Allen, you know, the movie where he's a court jester and says that line to the executioner. We were talking yesterday about recruiting Woody for our Advisory Council."

"Yeah, that is pretty obvious," I observed, "though I'm still not sure of what it means in this context. Carrie, you're the therapist."

"Well, a few things," she said. "Attempting to overthrow the King is very Oedipal, and since you're doing it with a group—which is obviously you guys—I suppose it symbolizes your political ambitions. Namely, to overthrow the current regime and replace it with one of our own."

"Wow," said Alice, "that's pretty good. I'm guessing you must have some very satisfied clients, up there in New York." Carrie went on.

"The head also represents intelligence, which is your most obvious characteristic, George. But you're also a deeply poetic person, a deeply feeling person, always quoting Goethe or Rilke or Nietzsche. So you're asking for a little off the top, i.e. a reduction in your analytical side so that your intuitive/emotional side can then come forward a bit more."

"Jesus Christ, Carrie, you're incredible," said Martin. "I guess my remark to George, that his dreams are my visions, now makes some sort of sense." Carrie continued.

"Woody Allen is also a person who is very neurotic, but he has managed to sublimate his neuroses into great creativity, in the form of a string of brilliant films. You, George, are a man caught between head and heart, between tradition and change, and that's a good thing: these conflicts finally resulted in a major breakthrough, namely the DI, the AP, and your entire post-GW career."

"That's a lot of initials," I said. Carrie ignored me.

"Finally, and perhaps most significant of all: the King admires you and seeks to learn from you. After all, you survived bodily death, which means you know certain things about the nature of survival. You did survive an assassination attempt, after all, and you are—at least in my opinion—a real survivor, George. You keep moving, you carry on, and you bring all of us along with you."

The whole thing left everyone out of breath. Finally Trevor said, "And I thought *I* was good at psychology. You're an absolute genius, Carrie."

"Carrie," I began, "this analysis seems to be spot-on, but in my experience, dreams often carry a message, telling the dreamer what they should do in their waking life. What do you think the message is, here? *Is* there one?"

"More than one, George. First, the dream is telling you to be a little less intellectual and a bit more intuitive and emotional. After all, you didn't tell the executioner to cut off your *entire* head. You said, "Just a little off the top." Stress on the word *little.* Head needs to pull back a bit, heart and guts need to come forward more. This will serve you, and your work, much better.

"Second, you are a survivor, and that's the wisdom that interests the King. In contemporary political life, it means that eventually, the state—the US government—might come to you for advice on how to survive. Then you'd have to decide whether to help them do it, or replace them. But the message for now is, just carry on.

"Finally, following up on neurosis as the source of creativity, the dream is telling you not to concern yourself too much with your inner conflicts. It's saying, as in the case of Woody, don't indulge those conflicts or neuroses, but rather use them, and allow them to do their work. This will result in an even greater creative output for you, and probably for the rest of the world.

"And George, I have to say this: I'm honored to be working for someone who would have a dream like this. Thank you for taking me on."

Once again, we all sat there as though hit on the head by a 2 x 4.

"Well," I finally said, "those are good messages. More heart, less head; carry on, survive; use my conflicts as fertilizer for creativity. Not bad."

"Hopefully the rest of us will also be able to survive bodily death," said Paola. "Jesumaria."

"Why do I have a feeling this dream is going to come back to haunt us?" Trevor mused.

"Let's hope not," I said. "But I do have to say, that if all of these events we have been living through were in a novel written by some sort of mental defective, I wouldn't be worried. I'd just enjoy the novel. Fortunately or unfortunately, these events are not fiction; they really did occur. It's just that it *seems* like fiction, don't you all think?"

And with that, I got up to help Alice with the dishes.

25.

Dear Alice,

I hope you can help me with my situation, which is very inauthentic. I don't know how to get out of it, but friends told me that the DI was very understanding. I'm stuck in an unhappy marriage with two small boys, ages 5 and 8. My husband isn't really interested in me or the kids; he works 10 hrs a day and then just comes home and watches TV. It's been nearly a year since we've had sex, or even a meaningful conversation. He's a good provider, and he doesn't mistreat me in any way; he's just checked out. I've suggested couples counseling to him, but he says it costs too much and is a waste of time.

You know, I studied art history in college, and then acquired secretarial skills and worked as a sec'y for a while until Howard "rescued" me. Things were pretty good the 1st 4 yrs, then slowly began to go downhill. I stay with him for the sake of the kids, but inside I'm dead. I don't think I can do this much longer. My parents say, "Hey, at least he provides for you, doesn't hurt you, and doesn't cheat on you"; but I feel they are from a generation for whom inauthenticity was the norm.

What should I do?

-Linda F.

Dear Linda,

Thank you for writing. Alice is deluged with work these days, so I hope you don't mind if I write you in her stead. My name is Carrie, I'm 40 years old, and I work professionally as a therapist.

Linda, all serious change is terrifying. There are practical issues to consider, and psychological issues to consider. On the practical side, you do have secretarial skills and could probably start checking out ads online today, to see what's out there in terms of jobs. I don't know your exact situation, but I'm wondering if you and the kids could stay with your parents or some relatives until you can get your feet on the ground.

On the psychological side, the problem is that although your situation is deadening and inauthentic, it's what you've gotten used to. Stepping into the unknown can be very scary. But I'll tell you this: almost every patient I've had has been able to make a significant change in their lives only when the pain of not changing became greater than the pain of changing. You may not yet be at that critical point; in which case, don't do anything. What I'm trying to say is, these are not intellectual decisions; they come from the gut. When it's time for you to leap, you'll leap.

God bless you, Linda, and feel free to write again.

-Carrie

Dear Alice,

I'm hoping you can give me some direction in my life. I'm a

25-year-old woman, with a B.A. in anthropology and a lot of experience in photography. Once I graduated college, it became clear to me that one couldn't work in anthropology without a Ph.D.; and although I sell my photos from time to time, it's not enough to pay the rent. Recently I got an admin job at a yoga studio, which I like because these are good folks: they hold classes on vegetarian cooking, the philosophy of yoga, environmental ethics, and other things that I believe in. But the pay is very low, and so I'm thinking I need to quit, and find a job as a waitress in a bar (where the tips are fabulous if you dress like a hooker), or as a lawyer's asst (which I've done in the past, and the salary is pretty good).

The problem is that I hate waitressing, and I hate lawyering, and therefore for me to do these jobs would be completely in-authentic. But they pull in a lot of $. When I do (study) anthro or photography or work for the yoga studio, it's completely authentic, and I'm very happy; but then I can't pay my rent. I'm torn, and it's driving me nuts.

Any ideas?

-Vanessa D.

Dear Vanessa,

Yours is a common dilemma: follow your heart and go broke, or follow the money trail, and feel miserable more than 40 hrs a week. By the way, most Ph.D.'s in anthro are driving taxis, as I'm sure you are aware.

I wish I could give you some sage advice, but it may come down to this: Which situation do you hate more? Of course, it may be possible—I don't know your exact circumstanc-es—to waitress or work as a lawyer's ass't half-time, earning enough to pay the rent but also giving you the time to take fotos and work at the yoga studio. That would probably constitute an authentic compromise. But if it's not possible, and you really do have to choose one or the other, then let me go out on a limb here: stay where you are. If you waitress or lawyer, you might eventually want to kill yourself. If you choose foto and yoga, what you will need to do is find a cheaper living situation, and eat vegetarian (which you probably already do). Yoga and photography are consciousness-expanding, and they could open doors for you. The other option is contracting; it will make you miserable in the end.

Of course, it's your choice, and I apologize for being presumptuous. But you asked for my thoughts, so there they are.

Namaste,

Alice

Dear Alice,

Here's the problem: I'm poor and homeless, and I don't see how authenticity can solve my problems. I am able to write you because the one friend I have bought me a membership in the DI ($5, you guys are great), and let me use his computer.

I sleep on park benches and sometimes in the doorways of alleys. I eat at soup kitchens, but I'm always hungry, and so I try to fish food out of garbage cans. I'm 44 yrs old, haven't been able to find work for the last 5 yrs (I was a janitor at a high school, and got laid off), and am lonely and miserable. The only thing I enjoy in my life is watching the guys play chess in Washington Square. I used to play myself, years ago.

-Brad D.

Dear Brad,

My name is Joan, I'm a therapist on the staff of the DI, and I'm filling in for Alice, who is overwhelmed with work these days. I hope that's all right.

To be honest, Brad, it seems to me that you *are* living an authentic life; crummy, but authentic. What I mean is, your life sucks, but you are able to admit that, to look reality straight in the eye. You didn't say anything about drugs or alcohol, so I'm guessing you have not taken those escapist routes. So in an odd way, you are ahead of the game.

Your problem, then, is not inauthenticity; it's being broke in a society that doesn't give a damn about those who have fallen on hard times. Since you have access to your friend's computer, I suggest you go all-out in searching the job lists on the Net. While you're doing that, however, I'd like to see if I can give you a leg up. Unlike the rest of American society, the DI and the AP *do* care about the fate of poor people, and as our membership has grown, we've created a network of folks willing to do what they can to provide real support. So here it is: You know Grace Church, Broadway and E. 11th St.? Well, the Rev. Bob Harkins is a member of the DI (we have done tons of outreach and lectures at churches and religious organizations across the country), and he may be able to offer you some p/t janitorial work. Print out this e-mail and take it to him. Bob is a very kind person, a truly authentic human being, and if he can help you, he will.

All the best, Brad; I have a feeling you're going to make it.

-Joan

P.S. Why not take up chess again, in the meantime?

Dear Alice,

I'm only 58 yrs old, but I have lung cancer and I'm dying. The doctors say I've got 6 months to live, at the outside.

Alice: I don't want to die. I feel like I wasted my life. I worked as an actuary, and it was boring. It was an inauthentic choice, which I now wish I could take back. You know, when I was in college, I was a math whiz. This was at Cornell, and the guy who taught Complex Variables had gotten his Ph.D. at age 19. So there I was, at 19, and guess what? I formulated a completely new theorem. My professor took me under his wing; he said he would get me into any grad school in the country, wherever I wanted to go. But my parents were dead set against it; they said college professors didn't make a lot of money, and I should become an actuary for a major insurance co. So instead of doing advanced calculus, I wound up doing stats and mortality tables, and I hated it.

I never got married, I never went to London or Paris, I never took up sketching or painting or guitar, and now I've got 6 months to live. I blew it. I lived a stupid, inauthentic life, and now I'm going to die.

-Roger F.

Dear Roger,

My name is Mark, I'm a therapist on the staff of the DI, sitting in for Alice, who has been a bit busy as of late. I hope you don't mind.

Roger, amigo, I wish I was there to give you a hug. Yours is indeed a heartbreaking story, and if I could wave a magic wand and take away your disease, I'd do it in a heartbeat.

All I can do is be practical with you. You remember that Jack Nicholson film, *The Bucket List*? I suggest you write down all the things you would like to do before you die, and try to do as many of them as you can in the next 6 months. Go to London and Paris; why not, after all? Sign up for a painting class. Ask a friend to set you up on a date, and take her to a fancy restaurant. Rent DVD's of great comedies, watch as many as you can, and laugh your head off. You get the idea.

You know, Roger, you "woke up" with 6 months left to live. Many Americans, perhaps most, don't wake up at all. At least you've got this. While you still can, say yes to life.

God bless you, my friend-

Mark

26.

Excerpts from George Haskel, *A Primer of Authenticity*

People who are authentic work with what's presented. They are in their lives as it is given; they do not sit around fantasizing about another life. Hope is not a big part of their psychology, because hope is always for something that's not in one's life right now. What it really is, is nostalgia for the future. The only futurizing you need to do, is to figure out what comes next in your life. This is what wisdom is.

People who are authentic take chances; they are willing, from time to time, to step into the unknown, or be guided by it. In the song by Green Day called "The Time of Your Life," the band says that when you come to a turning point in your life, just surrender. Time will grab you by the wrist, they say, and tell you where to go. It's unpredictable, but you can trust it. Whatever you wind up doing during your brief time on this earth, whether it's fighting injustice or teaching elementary school or running a furniture store, go with it; give it all you've got. Make sure you had the time of your life.

Howard Austen was Gore Vidal's partner, and they were together for a very long time. Howard died in his seventies. A short while before he died, he said to Gore: "It went by terribly fast, didn't it?" Take note, dear reader: I'm now seventy-one, and I can't believe it. It's like I blinked, and fifty years went by. What I wouldn't give to turn back the clock, and do it over again with awareness.

In his autobiography, Bertrand Russell wrote that his life had revolved around three things: love, truth, and the attempt to help those who had been hurt or crushed by the system. I find it hard to imagine a more authentic life.

One of the most authentic lives of the twentieth century was that of Mahatma Gandhi. Two of his most famous quotes:

"The world has enough for everyone's need, but not enough for everyone's greed."

"People ask me what is my message. I have no message. My life is my message."

Authenticity means above all, that you do not lie to yourself.

27.

Statements from political and military figures who switched over to the AP:

"During the next gubernatorial election, I intend to run on the Authentic Party ticket. I've come to the unavoidable conclusion that the two major political parties can do nothing for America or the American people, and in fact are not interested in doing anything for them."

—Jerry Brown, Governor of California

"George Haskel finally convinced me that if I voted for military appropriations that I didn't believe in, in order to stay in office, my life would be a sham. I intend to run for reelection on the Authentic Party ticket.

—Sen. Alex Robbins (D-NY)

"All the US military is doing is destroying other nations so as to benefit America, in terms of money and power. I served in Desert Storm and in the 2003 destruction of Iraq, and I'm ashamed of it. My exposure to the Authentic Party and its philosophy finally led me to resign my commission. As the influence of the AP spreads, perhaps other members of the armed forces will come to the same conclusion."

—Lt. Col. James Jacobs

"Thank God for the Authentic Party, and for my colleague Alex Robbins, who got me to study with George Haskel. Neither the Democrats nor the Republicans have any vision for America, because they are completely inauthentic. I'm switching over to the AP as of today."

—Sen. John Wilkinson (D-OR)

"I did a tour of Iraq as a gung-ho enlisted man in the Army, and what I wound up doing was killing innocent, unarmed civilians. I'm now working with the therapists at the Dullness Institute so that I don't kill myself as well. Fuck the Army, and fuck the system that supports genocide."

—Former Pvt. 1st Class _____ (name withheld by request)

"I served one term as a junior congressman, only to discover what a collection of clowns my colleagues were. You can't imagine how petty they are, the trivia that fills their professional lives. I shall run in the next congressional election on the Authentic Party ticket."

—Rep. Bill Riley (R-MI)

28.

So where are we, exactly? First, let me inform you that on August 8 of this year, the world's first authentic baby, Mario Enrico Jones, entered the world. His parents, Trevor and Paola, are raising him to be bilingual; they also intend to "raise him in authenticity." We wish them well.

Second: by that time, the DI/AP membership had reached the 4 million mark. In terms of grass-roots power, we had become a force to be reckoned with. As authenticity spread, we were in a position to start undermining the United States from within. The seminars, phone and e-mail service, local organizing, public lectures, Paola's mural—all of it had paid off. People knew who we were, and understood that we were offering a very different vision of America; and that we intended to seize power and implement that vision.

As for the Advisory Council for Restructuring America: a resounding success. Although we failed to get Woody Allen to join, the lineup incuded those already mentioned above, plus Susan Sarandon and Tina Fey. They must be true believers in the cause, because they went to no fewer than sixty-five major cities, holding forums on the rot that was destroying America, and what the AP intended to do about it. Most of these turned into town hall meetings, with people standing up and "testifying" about their own experiences, and in effect declaring their support for the AP. The combination of emotion and intellect was quite impressive.

When we next convened our Saturday morning breakfast meeting, there was a general feeling that it was time to roll out the big guns, go on the offensive, and call out the institutions that were the most inauthentic. We had hired two investigative reporters and two attorneys to assist us in this task.

"OK," said Trev, "it's gonna get ugly. Give me a category. Do you want to hit a major polluter, a major exploiter of labor, a major bank, Big Pharma, a manufacturer of nuclear weapons, big market chains, what? Give me your pet peeves, and let's draw up a list."

"Before we do that," Martin broke in, "I'd like to present you guys with a different list, which I've been working on for the past few days. This list is of where I'd like to see things wind up, on the eve of the next presidential election, OK?" Everybody nodded.

"Here goes. I'd like to see the DI philosophy sweep the nation. We now have 4 million members; I'd like to see it go to twice that, over the next two years.

"Second: as a result of the items on Trevor's hit list, i.e. our attack on corrupt institutions, I'd like to see them collapse. This will include:

a) Lots more politicians switch to the AP

b) Lots more military men denounce American imperialism and quit the armed forces

c) A number of major corporations fold

d) A number of media figures denounce hustling as a way of life

e) A kind of revolutionary fever grips the nation. Not of the Colton Farnsworth variety, but of the DI variety: the urgent feeling that the AP needs to replace the Republicrats and put the country on a whole new footing

f) A statement from George that if he's elected, he intends to apologize to every country we raped, from Mexico to Iraq, plus make amends in the form of substantial monetary reparations

g) A further statement from George that what really makes people happy is helping other people, not trying to defeat them or outdo them; that the American Dream was a mistake from the get-go; and that it was because of the Dream that we eventually turned into a genocidal plutocracy."

"Martin," I said, "we need to save f and g for after I'm actually in office. I just have a slight hunch that they won't fly with the American people, along with hanging Dick Cheney as a war criminal." Everybody laughed.

"That's probably right," said Trevor, "but nevertheless it's a good list. I'd just like to see things accelerate to the point that we have the power and the backing and the *cojones* to confront the present administration and tell them to step down."

"Wow," said Paola. "*That* would be a first, eh?"

"Actually, there's an interesting precedent here. Happened before my time, but I've been reading up on postwar American history, as part of my assignment."

"Assignment?" I questioned him.

"Sure," said Trev. "You told me, and I quote, to 'sit around and weave a huge web of mischief and intrigue.' So that's what I've been doing."

"Oh, *that* assignment. OK, weave away."

"The precedent is Watergate. There was a nationwide feeling that there was something rotten in the state of Denmark, until finally Nixon's position became completely untenable. Senior members of the establishment, such as Barry Goldwater, came to him and told him that for the sake of national stability, he had to go. Well, it had never happened before, that a sitting president resigned before his term of office was up, but that's what happened, and peace was restored."

"Well, yeah," I said, "but the guy was just replaced by a doofus, one who had the same ideology as Nixon but who wasn't also a crook. That's not really a regime change."

"True," said Trevor, "but it was nevertheless a first, of sorts, and so will this be. Hopefully there will come a time when a critical mass is reached, at which point we will be ready to say: 'Go, shmucks, or else.'"

"Or else what?" asked Martin.

"Not sure," replied Trevor, "but it will, or should, involve the threat of major political instability, once again. In fact, in this case, much more than just political instability."

"Jesus," I interjected, "I can't believe this is happening."

"Believe it, *jefe*. Everything up to now has been great—I've certainly enjoyed the ride—but it has also been playing paddy cake. Well, no more Mr. Nice Guy. Keep in mind that authenticity hardly excludes honest anger. Once we have the numbers, and the national sympathy, we'll be able to move. That's why I like items a through e on Martin's list."

The discussion went on all day long, once again in the spirit of the Sorbonne in 1968. In the end, we had to put aside Martin's list for a future time, and concentrate on Trevor's. The preferred target turned out to be Big Pharma, specifically the Lily Pad Corporation, whom we would sue for a variety of abuses: price fixing; inventing meds and then inventing diseases to go with them; making hundreds of billions in profits; bribing doctors to prescribe their products; finding ways around FDA prohibitions—and on and on. What we needed now was to sic our reporters on them, and then, our attorneys.

"To unleash the hounds of hell, is how Charles Dickens put it," I observed. "Or something like that, in any case. Our ultimate goal should be the actual breakup of the Lily Pad Corporation into a number of smaller, separate companies, with citizen watchdog groups keeping tabs on their behavior."

"Creative destruction," said Trevor; "the only way to go."

29.

The attack on the Lily Pad Corporation was a huge success. They were found guilty on all counts, and were required to pay the Authentic Party no less than $1 trillion in fines—an historical first. And they were subsequently broken down into a number of independent small companies, governed by citizen boards. They were, in short, smashed to pieces, and all of this was identified with the AP. As for the AP, we no longer needed the $5 subscription fees or Martin's money (in fact, his donations to us were returned to him, I'm happy to say; the guy is hardly a millionaire). A trillion dollars is a trillion dollars, after all. For five seconds, I contemplated buying a Lamborghini.

Our next target was a large market chain by the name of Flash-Mart. Its abuses were legion: crummy wages; severe regimentation and control of its employees, virtually turning them into robots; prohibition of unionizing; and the destruction of communities by driving small enterprises, stores, and whole neighborhoods out of business. This last item was not technically illegal, of course, but I suspect it figured into the judge's deliberations. Our lawyers certainly played it up as a prime example of how callous and destructive the Flash-Mart Corporation was. The trial went on for weeks, and in the end we won, to the tune of $1.5 trillion, this time. Flash-Mart folded, went completely out of business. I was interviewed in the aftermath by all the major media, and used the opportunity to make the following statement:

"Americans are increasingly coming to realize that everything is connected. It is inauthentic to shop at a place like Flash-Mart, just to save a few dollars on a sweater or whatever, when the result is the destruction of small, independent merchants in the community. And when the marketing giant pays its employees next to nothing, makes them behave like trained seals, and prohibits union organizing. I think the judge shared the Authentic Party's disgust at their behavior, and punished them accordingly.

"Corporations like Flash-Mart are legion in our society, a society based on hustling, competition, and exploitation. We at the Authentic Party have a very different vision of what life should be like, and we are hoping that the American people will give us a chance, when the next presidential election rolls around, to implement it.

"In the meantime, I'm hoping the American people will join me in saying to Wall Street, and the major corporations that are running this country: shame on you. You have poisoned the American soul, and body politic, long enough."

The speech precipitated widespread condemnation, and widespread praise. The battle lines were drawn.

Meanwhile, the victory over Flash-Mart brought in something like 2 million more members, as it became clear to many that cooperation and nonhustling was the wave of the future. Graffiti began to appear across the country, along the lines of "Join the AP, the party of fundamental decency," or "Want your soul back? Try the AP." We ourselves began to pay for billboard ads in literally every large city:

REAL AMERICANS NURTURE RATHER THAN HUSTLE

HUSTLING IS DISGUSTING

THERE IS NO WEALTH BUT LIFE

—etc. We appeared on radio shows, in public debates, in front of church groups, just about everywhere, hammering home the message that the American Way of Life was fundamentally sick, inauthentic, and that the AP intended to change all of that.

Defections—from the Dems and the GOP—began to multiply. We now had something like one-third of the Senate, and one-fourth of the House. And roughly 15 percent of American soldiers went on record denouncing American imperialism, and its effects at home and abroad. And then, the phone call I was not expecting, and never imagined would happen, came in: the Nobel Committee had awarded me the Peace Prize, and would be expecting me to attend the annual award ceremony in Oslo in December. The announcement stated, "To George Haskel, for his unrelenting efforts to humanize the United States, which has lost its way and become a force for evil in the world." Couldn't have put it better myself.

"Jesus fucking Christ!" screamed Martin at the next Saturday morning breakfast meeting. "The Nobel! The fucking Nobel!"

"Told you," said Trevor. "This, and continuing attacks on corporations and imperialism and hustling as a way of life, and we'll be in a position to ask the current administration to step down—*before* the presidential election."

DI membership was now past 8 million. The major media had begun to call the AP phenomenon, "the quiet revolution."

"I need to catch my breath for a moment," said Alice. "Will someone explain to me how this could be happening? I mean, hustling is buried so deeply in the American psyche, and is so pervasive throughout American culture..."

"Here's a possibility," ventured Paola. "What if Americans, at heart, are really decent folks, but over the decades got bent out of shape by a force that made them into something they were not? Sort of like a coil or a spring that got pressed down, farther and farther, until things came to a breaking point. Then George comes along at just the right moment, and says to them: 'You don't have to live like this, hating yourselves and your lives. You can have the lives you were meant to live.' And then: sproingg! All that repressed energy comes gushing out, George becomes a national hero, and the possibility of the US being a different sort of country emerges, seemingly out of nowhere. But this 'nowhere' had been building for some time."

"Or," said Trevor, "it might be a case of that choice I talked about long ago, when someone—George—triggers a nationwide case of existential strain. Some people—I almost did—react with anger and reject the whole thing, while others see a glimmer of light and on an impulse, decide to go with it. What about *that*? Human beings, after all, are not especially rational creatures. What any of them are going to do, faced with a serious dilemma, is hard to predict."

"Anyone care to make a prediction as to what the Chief Executive might do, faced with a demand that he leave office prematurely?" I asked.

"That's a foregone conclusion," Martin responded: "it'll be a big fat No."

"And then we'll do what?" said Alice.

"Beats me," I replied. "Happily, we have a bit of time to think this through."

Three days after the Nobel announcement, the DI office got a call from Woody Allen. He wanted to make a serious film about me, the DI, and the AP. Tentative title: "No Laughing

Matter." Would I come up to New York next week to talk to him about it? We set a date for lunch at a French restaurant in the West Village, the A.O.C.

Woody was already seated when I arrived. "Mr. Allen," I said, "this is really a great honor."

"For me, you mean," he replied; "you're the first Nobel Prize winner I've ever had lunch with."

I took a second to look around the restaurant. It was lovely: Old World feel, lots of wood, French posters on the walls. Was this where the beautiful people dined?, I wondered. Was I now beautiful? I turned back to Woody. He was wearing a tie (loosened) and sports jacket, and looked much like he did in his recent movies, i.e. old and young at the same time. He looked tired, and yet there was a twinkle in his eye. I tried not to gush.

"So tell me about this film you want to make," I began. "Your first documentary, I take it."

"Yeah, I'm hoping I can do a good job," he said modestly. "It will be about you, of course, but my real motivation is to create a propaganda tool for the Authentic Party—to help you win the next election." I smiled.

"My staff wants me to throw the current admin out of office prior to the election," I informed him.

"Hmm. A coup d'état," Woody mused. "This movie promises to be even more interesting than I expected."

The two of us ordered grilled fish, and Woody asked for an expensive bottle of Chardonnay. "This is on me, by the way," he said, "although I know you're now a trillionaire." He winked. "Really, George, I simply can't believe that this movement is happening; that you and your merry band are actually making a bid to turn this country around. Long overdue, in my opinion. I never say this in public, of course, but as an American, I'm embarrassed by what the US finally turned into."

"I'm glad you're on our side, Mr. Allen—"

"Woody, please."

"Woody. I'm just very happy you're in our camp. As for what happened to the United States, that's what I'm going to talk about in my Nobel acceptance speech."

"Well, I'll be there to film it," he said. "I also need to get clips from your encounter with Hillary—Jesus, that was hysterical—and Colton Farnsworth, and the Alexandria police. And of course, the assassination attempt."

"Makes sense," I said. "Could you pass the dish of lemons?" I squeezed one over my fish, and took a long pull of Chardonnay. "What about filming the DI team at my house in Takoma Park?" I suggested.

"Of course, of course," he said. "I want to give viewers a sense of the daily work, and also sit in on the Saturday morning meetings of the central group. Alice told me about it," he added, by way of explanation.

"Check out Paola Marini's mural as well. It is stored at the Swank Feinstein Gallery on West 57th Street, but I'm sure the curator will unroll it for you. It's also painted on a wall in San Francisco, if you feel like flying out there."

"Anything else?" he asked me.

"Well, I know you will be calling the film 'No Laughing Matter'—"

"Working title," he interjected. "If you have any other suggestions, let me know."

"Not particularly," I told him; "I was just thinking it might be nice to have some humor in the film. I mean, you *are* Woody Allen, and in addition, humor has been a big part of the DI since its inception. The Saturday meetings are often laugh fests. And I personally would feel bad if Americans came away thinking that the AP was some grim revolutionary machine. True, we're absolutely serious about what we're up to, but at the same time, we try not to take ourselves *too* seriously. It's an odd combo, and I hope you can capture it."

"I'll give it a shot. What else?"

"You might want to interview Jerry Brown, Senator Alex Robbins, and some of the military defectors to our cause. Perhaps also people in the steet, although I'm assuming that'll be a mixed bag."

"George, just to switch topics for a moment: How did all this happen? I hope you don't mind, but I spoke on the phone with some of your ex-colleagues at GW, and they are all fond of you, but they described you as a kind of Walter Mitty figure. One of them said, 'It's like suddenly discovering that a friend of yours happened to be Lenin.'" I chuckled.

"Damned if I know, Woody. You should talk to one of our team members, Martin Green. We were sitting around one day, and he explained to me Hegel's concept of the 'world historical figure.' I mean, no one is outrageous until they're outrageous, you know what I mean? Martin said that there were certain crucial turning points in history where history speaks through an individual, as with Lenin, for example, or Robespierre."

"Planning to chop off any heads?" he asked. Another wink.

"Just a little off the top," I said. Woody laughed uproariously. "God, that takes me back. I had forgotten all about that."

Some guy at the next table, in a dark suit, seemed to be eavesdropping. "Here's a bit of fun," I said. I went over to the guy.

"FBI or CIA?" I asked him. He was startled, thrown off. "You know," I said, "you can join us, be on the side of life. You don't have to be a douche bag forever." Flustered, the poor shmuck got up, asked for his check, and left the restaurant in a hurry.

"I'm going to see if we can't get that scene into the movie," said Woody.

"Anyway," I continued, "that's Martin's analysis. I don't know if he's right; in my case, it seems rather grandiose. Inside, I'm still just some guy teaching German lit at GW, and suffering through department meetings. I have a hard time putting myself in a league with Napoleon."

"And yet," said Woody, "you are the lightning rod for a very deep dissatisfaction that is now cresting in the US. This is why all this is happening. You came along and crystallized that dissatisfaction. Personally, I hope you go all the way. Let's face it: Americans treat each other like dogs, and maybe they are sick and tired of it. I sure am."

We finished eating, got up, shook hands, and parted. "I'll have my film crew out at your house this weekend," he said. "Just act natural, be yourselves."

Now how the hell are we going to do that?, I said to myself.

30.

So we held our normal Saturday morning breakfast meeting, but this time with Woody and his crew present, filming the whole thing. Woody told us to just have a typical discussion, and pretend no one else was present; but it was hard not to be self-conscious. Besides, when had we ever had a typical discussion? If we did, I certainly didn't remember it.

"OK, folks," I began; "let's hunker down. We're now on a pretty heavy trajectory, en route to a showdown with the White House. Trev, I've got two questions for you. First, when do you want to have it, and second, why in the world would the president agree to step down? Let's say we all show up there, with the Advisory Council in tow—perhaps this time with Woody accompanying us. [I gave Woody a sly look.] Why wouldn't the great man just tell us to go piss up a rope?"

"January 1st," replied Trevor. "And he won't be able to blow us off because in front of the White House will be 2 million Authentic Party members with pitchforks."

We all stared at him. "Wha?" I finally said.

"OK," said Trev, "here's the deal. There's a popular belief in this country that you can make revolutions with cell phones. The devotees point to Tahrir Square and the ousting of Hosni Mubarak, for example. But they never comment on the fact that the revolution fizzled out. 'Arab spring' became Arab winter; the final result of this so-called revolution is a military dictatorship. My point is that adolescents make 'revolutions' with cell phones, whereas adults use actual weapons. A number of commentators have pointed out that there were no cell phones during the French Revolution, which succeeded very well, thank you. Instead, pitchforks did the job. Not that I'm suggesting that we run the President through with a pitchfork, or stick his head in a guillotine. But the point is that if there are 2 million people outside the White House, with many of them holding pitchforks, and you tell him: okay, boychik, your time is up—well, what's he going to do? Order the army to fire on 2 million people? I mean, this ain't Kent State."

"There's something more surreal than usual about this discussion," said Martin. "First, where are we going to get 2 million people?"

"The membership now stands at 8 million," said Trevor. "Have you forgotten?"

"OK, so how do you plan to round them up?"

"By blanketing the newspapers and airwaves with news of the event, between now and January 1st. George could also mention it in his Nobel acceptance speech. Talk about publicity, eh? And then, of course, it'll take a while, but the office has the 8 million members on file, so we start phoning and e-mailing them all, as of today. And we have enough people on staff to do it. We also have huge amounts of cash in our bank account; $2 trillion buys a lot of advertising time, I'm thinking. Plastering major cities with fliers also wouldn't hurt."

"Trev," I put in gently, "I very much doubt that there are 2 million pitchforks in all of the United States."

"The real threat," he replied, "is warm bodies. The pitchforks are largely symbolic, but they say we mean business. What, then, is the president going to do, faced with 2 million warm, and potentially angry, bodies? I would, however, like to remind us all of George's dream of a few months ago. You all remember it, right? The one Carrie interpreted? Here's what she said, about the King coming to George for advice. Specifically, on advice as to how to survive. Our distinguished president will have no intention of stepping down, but he can't seriously order the Army to fire on 2 million people. They will refuse to do it, and once that happens, the jig is up. So what he'll do, George, is to try to make a deal with you. Here's my guess: he'll offer us lots of concessions, agree to all sorts of demands, but insist that he stay in office to carry them out."

"What sorts of demands do you have in mind?" Alice inquired.

"Remember Martin's list?" said Trevor. "Things like we apologize to all the countries we fucked over since 1848, and send them all massive reparations. Anyone got any other ideas?"

"A 100 percent tax on all annual income in excess of $500,000," said Paola.

"Excellent," said Trevor. "Hey, wait a minute," interjected Woody. We all laughed.

"Shipping Bush, Cheney, Wolfowitz, Rumsfeld and their ilk out to The Hague to be tried as war criminals," I put in, "and while we're at it, Bush Sr., Bill Clinton, and Mr. Obama." I was on a roll now, getting into the spirit of things.

"Those are probably good for starters," said Trev. "We can work on the list between now and January 1st, adding things like free medical care and education for all, food subsidies for the poor, dismantling the armed forces, putting numerous bankers and CEO's behind bars, and so on."

"Why not also insist that the president publicly announce he's a douche bag?" I suggested.

"I dunno, George," Martin responded; "I think he might have some resistance to that."

"But not to shipping the Bush administration off to The Hague?"

"Sure he will—object, that is—but we need to make demands that are justified, and that have real teeth to them," said Martin. "Although I certainly agree that the guy's a douche bag, and it would be great if he admitted it," he added. "But I have to say that in all my years of study of revolutions, I never ran across one that involved the head of state admitting he was a douche bag."

We discussed the douche bag issue at some length. I had the feeling this was for Woody's benefit.

"Anyway, douchebaggery aside," I finally said, "in keeping with my dream, and the matter of the King seeking to survive, I suspect Trev is right: he'll agree to a lot of our demands, maybe even most of them, so long as he gets to stay in office. We withdraw; the president then reneges on the deal. Meanwhile, we no longer have any leverage because the 2 million AP members have taken their pitchforks and gone home. Rounding them up a second time is probably unlikely, and in revolutions, timing is everything."

"He's right," said Martin.

"That's a real possibility," said Alice. "What will you do, George, if he says yes to our demands? Trust him? Or force the issue of resignation no matter what? Because that might mean calling on the crowd to storm the White House."

"Jesus, are we really having this discussion?" I asked no one in particular. "Hell, I don't know. I guess I'll have to cross that bridge when we come to it." It was becoming clear that everything would hang on my decision, and I wasn't happy with that. We were silent for a while.

Trevor finally spoke up. "OK, so here's the current agenda. The campaign to get the pitchfork crowd out on January 1st begins today. No. 2: George, you need to knock out your Nobel speech. No. 3—" Trev suddenly turned to Woody.

"Woody, I hope I'm not out of line here, but I suspect the release of your documentary would be of great help to us in this showdown. Any chance you could get it done before January 1st?" Woody shook his head. "Not realistically, Trevor; I'm sorry. Maybe by January 15, if we work on it pretty furiously."

The five of us looked at each other for a few minutes. "March 1st, then," said Paola. "That would also give us more time to contact the membership."

"I agree," said Alice; "March 1st."

"OK, *campañeros*," I said; "March 1st it is. Anything else? No? OK, I guess I'll do a bagel run. Woody, do you want yours with lox?"

31.

It was cold as hell when Alice and I arrived in Oslo for the award presentation of December 10. Also dark. In December, Oslo gets about six hours of light a day. We were whisked off to the Continental, a five-star hotel within walking distance of the City Hall, where the award ceremony would take place. It was truly luxurious, and Alice and I sank into the king size bed in our room. Tomorrow would be a day for walking and exploration, and then there would be the award ceremony the following day. I was grateful that I didn't have to be "on" right away.

Oslo is a city of about 600,000 people, and it is located right by a fjord. It's a mixture of old and new, with lots of sleek, modern architecture. It seems to radiate creativity, and enjoyment of life. Alice and I bundled up, got our cameras out, and then walked and walked. Waterfront views were spectacular, but we also enjoyed the market streets. It's a supremely civilized place. Subtract the winters and short days, I thought, and I could easily be persuaded to live here.

And so the fateful day came. Alice and I were escorted to the City Hall—functional architecture, they call it, completed in 1950—and into the auditorium, for my presentation. The head of the Nobel Committee made a brief introduction, while I looked out over the crowd, the sea of expectant faces. I took a few deep breaths. "Jesus, I hope this goes well," I said to myself.

I won't reproduce the entire lecture here; interested readers can easily locate it on YouTube. Let me just give you an abbreviated version.

Thinking About Fanaticism

By George Haskel

I want to talk to you about the problem of fanaticism, which seems to lie at the heart of many of the problems we have in the world today. Of course, the word itself, in these times, has become more or less equivalent to radical jihadism. We immediately think of Islamic terrorism; of ISIS, or al-Qaeda, for example, against which the United States is involved in a war without end—or so it seems. But one thing I have learned, as an American citizen, is that the US never looks at its own fanaticism, and indeed, never regards any of its actions or ideologies as fanatical. We in America never talk about capitalist fanaticism, for example, or neoliberal fanaticism, and can't seem to understand how fanatical they really are. Yet, in the promotion of this ideology, along with the attempt to project our way of life—the so-called American Dream—into every corner of the globe, we destroy entire nations. We butcher and massacre innocent, unarmed civilians, and think nothing of it. Everyone must be like us; everyone must get on the bandwagon of the hustling way of life.

The problem is that hustling is really the religion of More, and so it is empty at the center. After all, if your goal is More, you can never have enough. But this is hardly genuine spirituality, and it violates the call to moderation endorsed by virtually every religion on the planet, not to mention Aristotle and Lao-Tse. And because it provides no real satisfaction, or peace of mind—just the opposite, in fact—Americans feel haunted. They feel they are dead, in some way, which is actually true, and war is the easiest way to feel alive—the ultimate adrenaline rush. Because of our emptiness, millions die, seemingly without end.

The great American historian C. Vann Woodward, as early as 1953, wrote that any society fixated on a single economic regime or ideology was doomed to fail. It didn't matter if it was Southern slavery or Northern laissez-faire capitalism, in the long run it had no future. I don't know if I, just a single individual, can save the United States; among other things, the hour is rather late. Nor do I know why I was chosen for this historical role. But I do know this: on March 1st of next year, in Washington, DC, millions of members of my political party, the Authentic Party, will gather outside the White House, and I will enter it with my trusted friends and advisers. And I will ask the president, who is perpetuating this murderous regime, and this destructive, monolithic ideology, to step down, so that I may be given the opportunity to turn things around. If he should refuse, I can't predict the outcome; but with hopefully 2 million people gathered outside, demanding a regime change and a change of ideology, I can venture to guess that the outcome won't be to his liking. So I am hoping that the president will have the wisdom to do the right thing. He is not a bad man, nor is he a deliberately evil man. But he is a very foolish man, and like his predecessors, he perpetuates a way of life that is destructive, anti-human, and yes—fanatical.

As for our demands, they are many, including things such as sending the former Bush administration officials off to The Hague to be tried as war criminals. Other things include free medical care and education, such as exists in Norway. I don't need to list them all at this time. But the demand that is at the top of our list is that the president leave office, endorse the changing of the guard and my right to succeed him, and permit the Authentic Party to bring decency and authenticity back to America. Although nearly everything the president has done in office up to now has been foolish, I and the membership of the AP—now more than 8 million people—are praying that with respect to this one decision in his life, he renounce the path of foolishness.

Thank you.

Well, the reader is well aware, by now, of the uproar this lecture precipitated. Being foolish, the president put the Army on full military alert. Most American newspapers didn't know how to react. After all, we now had many politicians on our side—ones who praised and endorsed my speech. Referring to the president, the *Baltimore Sun* ran an editorial entitled "Dump the Jerk!" The *New York Times*, on the other hand, said Haskel was "completely off his rocker." European papers from London to Vienna basically said it was time for the US to stop ruining the world under the phony banner of democracy. But the major focus now, worldwide, was what was going to happen on March 1st. I was wondering about it myself, perhaps more than most.

I got a call from Woody on January 18: the film was finished, and he wanted to invite the central group of the DI to come up to New York for a private screening he had arranged at a theater in Tribeca, four days from then. We decided to include Carrie, already in New York, along with Paola; so it meant taking the bulletproof car once again, picking Martin up in Baltimore, and then making our way to Manhattan. Woody was planning to start distribution of the film shortly after that, so we were all excited, as well as a bit nervous. This would be a major pitch for the March 1st event; a lot depended on how we came off to the general public.

As it turned out, we didn't have to worry. Sitting in the

darkened theater, the six of us were increasingly relieved as Woody portrayed us not as a bunch of lunatics, but the rest of the country, in particular the government, as a bunch of lunatics. He showed how we helped the poor, counseled our membership on the authentic life, spoke out against war and hustling—the list went on and on. He did interviews with Bill Maher, Jerry Brown, Sherry Turkle, Philip Roth, Tina Fey, Julia Louis-Dreyfus, and other "stars" who had joined the AP camp. Finally, he wound up the film with that initial Saturday morning discussion we had on confronting the president on March 1st. Then the camera zeroed in on Susan Sarandon, who didn't mince words: "Many Americans are fed up with the American Dream and the American Way of Life. We are fed up with the bullshit, the inauthenticity, not to mention the genocide perpetrated in our name. We wait for March 1st with dread and anticipation, hoping that the president has the intelligence to step aside, and let George Haskel take the helm. In a word, the time for 'business as usual' is over."

The lights went up. The six of us looked at each other and smiled.

"I take it that's a yes?" said Woody.

"*Alea iacta est,*" said Alice.

"Hey, I know my Caesar," Woody replied. We all went out for dinner.

The reception of the film: ah, gentle reader, you know this as well. Complete national hysteria. The *Sacramento Bee* ran a headline that said, "Revolution on March 1st? Long Overdue!" Bill Maher announced that he was on the Advisory Council and would be at my side when I confronted the president. He added that he particularly enjoyed the discussion in the film of the president as a douche bag. The *New York Times* called for our immediate arrest, and *Washington Post* editorials down to February 28 ranted and raved against us to the point of incoherence. Meanwhile, the AP membership deluged us with e-mails, saying, "Great movie!" and "I'll be there on March 1st, count on it!"

And so, incredibly, the day arrived.

32.

We got there on February 28. Alice had booked us some suites in the Sofitel, on Lafayette Square; the Advisory Council would be staying there as well. Outside, the crowds had already gathered, and yes, many people were holding pitchforks. "How in the world did this happen?" I asked myself. "I must make a note to kill Trevor."

The six of us (including Carrie) met in my and Alice's suite, and ordered room service for lunch. "Well," said Martin, "how are you feeling, George?"

"Feeling," I repeated, mostly to myself. "Hmm. I have a feeling I might not live to see March 2. That's how I'm feeling."

"George," said Trevor, "we may not get 2 million out there tomorrow, but I think we can count on at least a million. You'll be flanked by all of us, not to mention Woody, Tina, Susan Sarandon, Bill Maher, Philip Roth, and the rest of the Advisory Council. The president won't refuse us an audience; that would be too risky for him, politically speaking. You start out by asking him to step down, and then take it from there. You've got our list of demands all printed up, and in any case, they have been on the front page of most newspapers around the world for the last month. This is going to be a win, Mr. President, and I think we all need to start addressing you like that from now on." I waved my hand, shook my head.

"Oh, Trev, sometimes I don't know whether to hug you or hit you." Suddenly, I began to sob. It must have been the cumulative effect of all the tension that had been building up over the past year, but I sat in my chair and bawled my eyes out. Alice pulled her chair up next to mine and put her arms around me. I cried and cried, and it went on for twenty minutes. Meanwhile, everyone else came over and hugged me as well.

"George," said Carrie, "are you aware that you are the most courageous person on the planet? Millions worldwide respect you, adore you, and are cheering for you. Do you know that?"

"I guess," I blubbered. "It's that I just don't know how I got here, is all. One day I'm giving Alice a load of bullshit at a café in Morelia, and the next day—which is what it seems like—I'm the spearhead of a major revolution. Me! I'm just a little nebbish teaching Goethe to bored undergraduates!"

"Hardly," said Paola. "You are a man of incredible vision, incredible courage, and as Carrie says, millions of people are now hoping you will succeed."

I cried some more. Finally, the other four left us, and Alice and I stretched out on the enormous bed and made love. After, she said, "Do you know how happy I am, that you fed me a load of shit in Morelia? That turned out to be the most important day of my life."

I spent the evening reading Heinrich von Kleist and making notes for tomorrow's audience with His Lordship. I didn't sleep very much. At 11 A.M., as agreed upon, the Advisory Council came to my suite, along with Martin, Carrie, Trev, and Paola, and we began the walk to the White House.

It was a brilliantly sunny day—a good omen, perhaps. And—*mirabile dictu*—it did look like there were 2 million people out there, maybe more. The crowd parted for us as we walked across Lafayette Park, and up to the front door of the White House.

"Ready, muchachos?" I said to them. Everyone nodded.

The president met us at the door. "You know why we are here, Mr. President."

"I do, George," he replied. "Perhaps we could all gather in the Oval Office."

There were a fourteen of us, one of him. Chairs were brought in. We all sat down, the president behind his desk. "I'll give it to you in a word, George: No. I'm not stepping down."

"I've got 2 million people out there, Mr. President. If you don't there'll be hell to pay."

Bill Maher spoke up. "You've seen Woody Allen's film, Mr. President, right? Well, we're here to tell you that this is no laughing matter."

The president looked at me instead. "Listen, George, I've got your list of demands; it's been published a million times by now. And I'm willing to play ball with you. In fact, it might surprise you, but I'm willing to send Cheney and his goons off to the World Court. I'm actually willing to meet most of these demands. But I am *not* willing to step down. So the demands get met, but I'm the one who is going to meet them. Agreed? Then we can all shake hands and go home. If you refuse, things are going to get very tense around here."

"Tense for *you*, Mr. President," said Philip Roth. "All George has to do is go outside and tell the 2 million people out there that you refused to step down, and you're history."

The president laughed. "Really? What will actually happen is a bloodbath, Mr. Roth, with all of you dead, and me still in office at the end of the day."

"So you are willing to have your troops out there fire on the crowd?" I asked him. "What kind of presidency will you be left with, after that? And what if they refuse to fire, which could very well happen? What then?"

"That's a chance I'll have to take. I'm not leaving this office quietly; I can tell you that."

"You're bluffing, Mr. President," said Trevor. "You simply can't be that stupid."

Again, the president looked at me. "Try me," he suggested. We glared at him for a minute or so: the ultimate standoff.

"Look, George, here's the deal. All of this is now up to you; it's all in your hands. We are going to clear out of here and leave you in the Office for one hour. You have one hour to decide whether you want to accept my offer, or go outside and tell your minions to storm the Winter Palace. Choose wisely, George. I'll be back in exactly one hour to get your decision. Everybody out now," he announced rather loudly. They all left.

33.

And so there I was, alone, sitting in the presidential chair, looking out at the view. It was a great view, the Washington Monument and all, reminding me of the Founding Fathers, and how differently the nation had evolved from what they originally had in mind.

And I thought: I guess I never knew it, but my entire life has been leading up to this point. I looked around the room. It reeked of authority, of dignity.

What to do? I kept going back and forth between the two possibilities. I thought of the talk I gave at the UN, about the need to act: "The Choice Before Us Today." Was the president bluffing? Or, if I declared war, would he actually start murdering hundreds of people—myself and all the people I loved included? The guy was clearly a sociopath.

What to do?

I thought of my dream, and that silly line, "just a little off the top," and Carrie's interpretation, about relaxing my intellect and letting my intuitive side come forward. And suddenly, out of nowhere, the last stanza of Philip Larkin's fabulous poem, "High Windows," popped into my head:

"Rather than words comes the thought of high windows:
The sun-comprehending glass,
And beyond it, the deep blue air, that shows
Nothing, and is nowhere, and is endless."

And just like that, I knew what I had to do.

ABOUT THE AUTHOR

Morris Berman is a poet, novelist, essayist, social critic, and cultural historian. He has written thirteen books and more than 150 articles, and has taught at a number of universities in Europe, North America, and Mexico. He won the Governor's Writers Award for Washington State in 1990, and was the first recipient of the annual Rollo May Center Grant for Humanistic Studies in 1992. In 2000, *The Twilight of American Culture* was named a "Notable Book" by the *New York Times Book Review*, and in 2013 he received the Neil Postman Award for Career Achievement in Public Intellectual Activity from the Media Ecology Association. Dr. Berman lives in Mexico.

ALSO AVAILABLE FROM
THE OLIVER ARTS & OPEN PRESS

FICTION

THE DECLINE AND FALL OF THE AMERICAN NATION, Novel by Eric Larsen (2013)

THE END OF THE 19TH CENTURY, Novel by Eric Larsen (2012)

THE BLUE RENTAL, Texts by Barbara Mor, (2011)

ABLONG, Novel by Alan Salant (2010)

KIMCHEE DAYS, Novel by Timothy Gatto (2010)

TOPIARY, A Modular Novel by Adam Engel (2009)

NONFICTION

DANCE WITHOUT STEPS, Memoir by Paul Bendix (2012)

THE SKULL OF YORICK, Essays on the Cover-up of 9/11 by Eric Larsen (2011)

AFGHANISTAN: A WINDOW ON THE TRAGEDY, by Alen Silva (2011)

I HOPE MY CORPSE GIVES YOU THE PLAGUE, Essays by Adam Engel (2010)

HOMER FOR REAL: A READING OF THE ILIAD by Eric Larsen (2009)

FROM COMPLICITY TO CONTEMPT, Essays by Timothy Gatto (2009)

POETRY

A CROW'S DREAM, Poetry by Douglas Valentine (2012)

THE BOOK OF TRANSPARENCIES, Poetry by Gregory Marszal (2012)

LISTENING TO THE THUNDER, Poems by Helen Tzagoloff (2012)

THE EXPEDITION SETS OUT, Poetry by Alan Salant (2011)

AUTUMN LAMP IN RAIN, Poetry by Han Glassman (2011)

CELLA FANTASTIK, Prose Cartoons by Adam Engel (2011)

I AM NOT DEAD, Poetry by Gregory Marszal (2010)

Oliver titles are available through any bookseller or at
www.oliveropenpress.com

We hope *The Man Without Qualities* inspires you to look at other Oliver titles.

How did you hear about us? Would you recommend this and/ or other Oliver titles to a friend?

Did you purchase this title online, from one of the "usual online dealers," or from the Oliver website?

Did you find this title in a local bookstore?

Please contact us about this book and other Oliver titles you might have read.

Email Oliver's editor and publisher, Eric Larsen:
editor@oliveropenpress.com
or Oliver's associate editor, Adam Engel:
assoceditor@oliveropenpress.com

You can also reach the press by mail:
The Oliver Arts & Open Press
2578 Broadway, Suite #102
New York, New York 10025

Lightning Source UK Ltd.
Milton Keynes UK
UKHW021022200820
368550UK00018B/2038